"'The other day I was lounging on the c[...] newspaper,' wrote Beth Boswell Jacks in one of her *Snippets* stories. You get that feeling every time you read one of her columns: Here is a warm, articulate Southern lady sitting down to chat with you about all her fascinating experiences and all her intriguing thoughts. Jacks is one of those Deep South writers whose works have a distinctive regional flavor but transcend the South to appeal to people of all regions and all persuasions. She's a gentle kind of writer who can dissect an issue without drawing blood. Enjoy her writing with your morning coffee, your afternoon tea or your evening whatever. It will enhance the experience."
— Gene Owens, columnist, *Greasepit Grammar*

"Beth Boswell Jacks writes with wit, originality, and insight. Readers can get a valuable education from reading her columns too. Thanks to Jacks, I now know when my wife should not wear her diamond jewelry ('Sparkle Plenty Bombs') and her watch."
— C. Tolbert Goolsby, Jr., Author of *Sweet Potato Biscuits and Other Stories*

"Beth Jacks looks at the humorous side of life and is just the ticket for a little stress relief. She teaches us how to take life not so seriously, while touching on quirky, funny subject matter. As a newspaper columnist myself, I read her stories and then say to myself, 'I wish I had thought of that for a column and could convey such wit.'

"Our readers tell us they turn to her column because they know it will be fun and lift their spirits. We get a lot of positive feedback on her writing, showing that people want something that is a break from the often grim, depressing news in a newspaper. She's the real McCoy."
— Chris Wilson, journalist, *The Amory Advertiser*

"A couple of years ago I received a package of columns from Beth Jacks, a resident of Cleveland, Miss. I get packages like this often– wannabee newspaper columnists.

"The rest is history. I was one of the first newspapers to publish her columns. They have a down home feel and are excellent—Erma Bombeck from the South, if you will. They are like hot apple cider in front of a nice fire, with your house shoes on, on a cold winter night. They also can be funny and have the ability to provide the warm and fuzzy we all need in our lives."
— Mark Boehler, Editor, *Daily Corinthian*

"Beth has done a superb job with *Snippets*. She offers homespun humor that brings back fond memories for our readers."
— Mark Williams, Editor & Publisher, *The Bolivar Commercial*

"Beth's columns make fun reading because she's always ready to laugh at herself and then move on from there, lifting the ordinary to a new and unique perspective or reducing the pompous with a few strokes of common sense."
— John Howell, Publisher, *The Batesville Panolian*

Snippets

by
Beth Boswell Jacks

Cork Hill Press
Carmel

CORK HILL PRESS™

Cork Hill Press
597 Industrial Drive, Suite 110
Carmel, IN 46032-4207
1-866-688-BOOK
www.corkhillpress.com

Trade Paperback Edition: 1-59408-225-1

Printed in the United States of America

1 3 5 7 9 10 8 6 4 2

For G-Man

CONTENTS

U~

W~

X~Y~Z

FOREWORD

I've been given one page in this book, which only seems right since I've been the source of much of Miz Snippet's merriment.

I first met this author when I was five years old—or so she says.

Her story is that my mother, one of the pillars of the First Methodist Church in Cleveland, Mississippi, paid a visit to the Boswell family soon after they moved to town. According to the author's memory, my mother had me in tow.

Of course, I recall none of that, but I've never doubted it. If the author remembers me at age five, I remember her.

What I do remember is this delightful, smart, friendly, and compassionate girl who caught my attention at age thirteen or so.

Somehow I thought we might have a future together. After all, she could write, I could not, and she offered to help me.

And help me, she did. Those boring English assignments I submitted without her help got me my consistent "C" or worse. With her help, I received "B+" on several papers and an occasional "A." So, our relationship showed promise at an early age.

The stories she shares are true and endless. I know, because we have spent virtually our entire lives together.

From age sixteen to the present, she has been my constant companion, my best friend, my lover, and my inspiration. I cannot imagine life without her.

And she makes me laugh. You'll laugh, too, and maybe even shed a tear. Be forewarned by this foreword.

—Gerald H. Jacks (aka G-Man)

A Chilling Afternoon

I'm with hubby G-Man on a business trip. He's gone all day to do whatever it is people do on business trips, and I'm left to my own whims and delights. Shall I sleep late? Shall I read? Shop? Eat big fat slabs of cheesecake while he's not around to scold me?

I do all of the above, then set out on my mission. It's too cold to go, but I'm going anyway. I hail a taxi.

"Want to go highway or local?" the driver asks me.

I tell him "local" because I want to see all the city I can. We've got plenty of highways back home in Mississippi, I tell him, then pose the standard Southern question: "Where you from?"

"Bangladesh," he says, "and, guess what, I've been to Mississippi."

I show my surprise, and he says, "I worked for World Com before everything crashed to hell. Went to Mississippi to our headquarters several times. I'm driving this taxi right now till I can find another job."

He zips us through the city at a clip any NASCAR driver would envy. We head south on Lexington Avenue, dodging cabs, vans, trucks, and bundled pedestrians. The temperature is hovering in the low 20s, and even these yankee folks are cold, heading to wherever they're going with their heads bent against the icy wind.

We reach Gramercy Park. It's deserted because of the freezing temp—no mothers with babies in strollers, no lounging office workers, no homeless. Everybody's racing someplace or they're staying put inside.

We turn on East 21st Street, then Park Avenue. Norah Jones is singing on the radio. What a voice!

We come to Union Square and I spot one shivering soul, an artist sitting on the concrete steps, sketching something. Drawing the skyline, maybe; I don't see anything else of interest. Everywhere there are the ubiquitous delis and pizzerias—nothing worth braving the frigid air to draw.

We're stalled in traffic beside another cab. While my driver Romie and I chat, I observe the neighboring taxi driver clipping his fingernails. I wonder what his passenger is thinking. I don't believe taxi drivers in the South do such a thing.

We start up again and pass Canal Street, Duane Street, Warren Street, several more, then turn right on Fulton. Romie stops at the next corner.

"Here you are," he says. I pay, offering a nice tip and thanks. I tell him to be sure to visit Mississippi again. I add, "Soon, y'hear?"

I get out of the cab. The cold causes me to catch my breath—or maybe it's not the freezing temp at all. Tears fill my eyes. Is it the bitter cold or is it the fence filled with flowers and banners and poems and pictures that looms in front of me like a badly designed stage set?

I look across the street. A twelve foot iron lattice fence is there, surrounding a deep, gargantuan pit. I cross the street, my heart pounding, and, once again, I have to catch my breath.

In the pit are cranes and backhoes and workers in thick jackets, mufflers and hard hats. A smell of smoke hangs in the air. Several buildings are covered in plastic. A dozen American flags wave in the wind, and a big sign says, "Never forget!"

People in heavy coats, caps and gloves, are milling, reading signs on the fence, absorbing the raw emotion of the place. I wonder how many of these folks lost loved ones here.

My heart is full as I walk around the fence enclosed pit. I'm numb with cold and horror as I think of the devastation and loss of life. I wonder how this could have happened.

After thirty minutes of walking I'm almost frozen, so I slip into a Starbucks to get some coffee and reflect on what I've seen. While I jot notes and sip the hot brew, I realize I'm hearing Ray Charles singing "Unchain My Heart" over the speakers in the café.

"Unchain my heart," he sings, "and set me free . . ."

That's it, I think. The hearts of all of us in this whole world need unchaining, the only way we can ever be free from distorted ideas about each other. We need unshackling from preconceived notions. From hate and distrust.

I finish the coffee and brave the cold once again to catch a taxi back to my hotel. I jab a gloved thumb in the air and a merciful driver pulls up immediately. I jump in, edgy and bewildered.

"Please, Lord, unchain our hearts, every single one of us," I mutter, taking one last look back as we pull away from Ground Zero.

A Word from Miz Chili Pepper

I once wrote a column reminding fashion conscious women that proper etiquette dictates NO diamonds or other precious jewels should be worn during daylight hours.

The story received quite a few comments—mostly from folks who had never heard of such a thing. Well, they obviously didn't take home economics in the eighth grade under the tutelage of Mrs. Moses and Mrs. Peacock—no wonder they never learned the Jewelry Laws.

But the unenlightened were joined by a few readers like my childhood pal Ann. She sat by me in home ec class and should have retained such important knowledge, but responded to that column by writing: "Hey, where was I? Baking biscuits? I don't remember that."

Perhaps Ann was hem-stitching her purple apron. I don't know. I didn't dream up that aesthetic edict; I may exaggerate every now and then, but I never prevaricate. Well, rarely.

Because of the wild success of that column and its educational value, I've kept an eye open for other tidbits of fashion news I can pass along to appreciative readers. This morning I read something info-rich in the Miss Manners column and thought: Yes! This will go out to Snippets World immediately.

And what would that info be?

Just this: We women can't wear red or white or black to weddings. That's correct.

I knew black was taboo for joyous occasions—too closely associated with mourning—although I think we've all decided we can wear black any ole time we want, especially when we need to project the illusion we've shed a few pounds. Or when we don't have another thing we can wiggle into and top with a string of pearls.

I also knew white was out. Can't compete with the bride, you know.

Then again, one of the most popular trends in recent years has been for bridesmaids to wear cream or white. If the bride's girlfriends can promenade down to the front of the church looking like the bride, why can't we guests? No good reason really, except we know what white does to us—we look pasty and our pantyhose line shows. Yeah, let's forget white.

But red? What's the problem? Too flashy, maybe, as in, "Hey, don't look at the bride; look at ME. I am one decked-out floozie!"

And remember, red is associated with scarlet women, chili peppers, and traffic lights (STOP!)—none of which we want to think about at weddings.

Several years ago I made a roadtrip to the northeast corner of Tennessee with two longtime friends to attend a wedding. As we cruised the miles, we three gabbed nonstop, discussing lots and lots of things—including an analyzation of why we dress the way we dress.

Friend #1 admitted she dressed to please men, sort of Sweet Potato Queenish. Friend #2 claimed she dressed to please women, a la Katie Couric. And me? We decided I dress to please me—Janet Reno, maybe.

(Give me loose and comfy. I avoid anything scratching, binding, or choking. I figure if God had wanted us in uncomfortable clothes, he'd have vetoed the fig leaves and put Adam and Eve in corn shucks.)

Yep, on that jaunt to the mountains of Tennessee we three women talked about everything under the sun . . . almost. Too late now, I discover my fashionable friends failed to pass on some really important information—like about not wearing red, black, and white to weddings.

Wouldn't have mattered though.

You may think I'm fashion savvy 'cause of my pressed jeans and my vast knowledge of proper etiquette, but I was smart enough to realize the men at that wedding were all looking at Friend #1 and the women were all eyeing Friend #2. Nobody was giving me a second glance as I led our threesome down the aisle in my little black suit, low-heeled shoes, flashy red scarf and, why sure, pearls.

Fashion sense is elementary, my dears.

Hang around with folks who dress to please other people, let all the attention go to them, and, quite literally, you can pretty well suit yourself.

Back In The Doo Wop Days

When I tell folks writing has been my passion since childhood, I'm not just spoofing.

In fact, I have my diaries from 1957 - 1963 to prove it, for rarely a day went by that I didn't meticulously record the events of my semi-exciting teenage life. I've even thought about writing a book about this era based on my diaries, but decided the editing of sensitive material would trigger a stroke or divorce, and I don't care for either.

A recent camping weekend brought back memories of a summer trip decades ago, sending me to the diaries in search of my account of this weekend in that north Mississippi paradise. I found that entry and more.

Some editing has been done to protect the guilty.

It was the summer of 1960.

JUNE 1 - Dear Diary, today is the start of my sixteenth summer. Hope it's better than last year. I went to town this afternoon and bought a bathing suit at Sterling's. Cost $20. If Daddy knew it cost that much he'd have a fit. Delia had a cyst removed from her tongue today. I'm spending the night with her. We're watching TV because she can't talk.

JUNE 5 - MJ and Ann picked me up in "Old Gray." It's a bucket. We went to see "Don't Eat the Daisies." Funny show, but then we had a flat. We left the car (nobody would want it) and walked home.

JUNE 6 - Daddy says the Olivers are going to let us use their cabin at Lake Enid next weekend. Wonder if they have cute boys over there.

JUNE 11 - We're at Enid. Two boys are flirting with Kak and me. One is blond and one is black-headed. They're tall and very tan. Their names are

Johnny (or maybe it's John) and Bird (maybe Brad). They talk kinda fast . . . [edit edit edit]

JUNE 14 - Watched the men paving our street today. It's a mess. So is my life. Listened to Randy's Record Shop on the radio tonight. I love Elvis's slow songs.

JUNE 18 - Delia's grounded. Her parents say she doesn't help around the house enough. They also found out we'd been chasing the mosquito truck. That's why I ran into that sign and scratched their car up. This is some boring summer.

JUNE 20 - There are no words to say how crummy I feel.

JUNE 21 - Bill H. asked me for a date for Saturday night. Gosh, life is great!

JUNE 22 - I took little Melanie to see "My Dog Buddy" tonight. We both cried. A man and some dogs did tricks before the show, which was fun—but then the show was real real sad. Another reason Mel cried was because Mama lent Pepper to a lady to mate with her dog and Melanie wanted to know where Pepper went. Mama couldn't tell her, so Melanie cried and Mama's going to get Pepper back tomorrow. I don't know if he's finished or not.

JUNE 25 - Bill H. and I had a wreck! He lives in the country and didn't know about the stop sign on Maple. A truck knocked us into the Smith's yard. I was so shook up I didn't write in you. (This is tomorrow.)

JUNE 28 - We had a swimming party tonight. A sharp girl from Iowa with one eye was there. She said we have neat kids. I have a crush on Mike.

JUNE 29 - Gerald asked me to go to the show Saturday. I don't have a crush on Mike any more. I'm not going to fall for Gerald though. I think what I want to do with my life is be a nightclub singer or something. I think I've outgrown boys.

Pretty deep stuff, huh?
Well, in spite of my best intentions I fell for Gerald (the G-Man), married

him six years later, and still hold his hand when I go to sleep at night. Pepper is long gone, I decided against becoming a nightclub singer, we never saw Johnny and Bird again, and to this very day I love Elvis's slow songs.

Ahhh, what memories!

Back in the doo wop days . . . we had a ball . . . time just slipped away . . . back in the doo wop days.

Beauty Queen Wannabe

In spite of the fact that I had two of the best looking legs in the whole high school (circa 1960), I was never a beauty queen.

There was a real problem from the waist up. The difficulty started in the chest area and continued to the tip of my head. I wasn't charm-less, but let's just say there were a few obstacles to overcome before I could walk across a stage and be crowned Miss Anything.

To compound matters, this . . . umm . . . mattered. I truly wanted with all my heart to be a beauty queen. As a matter of fact, some of my best friends were beauty queens. They had the tiaras and sashes hanging on their pink walls to prove it. I had piano certificates, which carried nowhere near the same importance.

I remember sprawling on the floor at Margaret and Dean Pearman's house in the summer of 1960, eating pineapple sherbet and watching Lynda Lee Meade crown Mary Ann Mobley as the next "Miss America." Or was it the other way around?

Anyway, Mary Ann and Lynda Lee cried for joy while I cried with the ragged anguish only a teenager can feel. The grownups thought I was weeping with excitement for our two Mississippi winners, when actually I was wishing the beauty queens had my bumps on their rosy cheeks and I had their scepters.

It never worked out that way, but over the years I came to realize that they had probably had their share of bumps too. And tears. So all's well that ends well. I guess.

Why am I wading through all this? Because I've just read something that makes me think my beauty queen chances may not have completely slipped away.

The Mississippi coast recently hosted a big pageant (well, not that big—only 2 contestants this year, but it's sure to grow) where "mature" women vied to be crowned Ms. Mississippi Senior.

Hey, that's not all. The winner gets to go on to the national pageant in Reno sometime in November. How 'bout that?

This year's winner, a 79 year old cutie, performed an original comedy sketch, edging out the other contestant who danced and twirled her straw hat to a lively Cajun tune. Lord knows, the judges must have had to wrestle with that decision.

If any of the rest of you missed out on being beauty queens in your younger days, call me. I'll find out how we can take the 2004 Ms. Mississippi Senior pageant by storm, which we most certainly would. Our time has come.

Fact is, this isn't the only senior pageant in this good ol' USA, where no less than 700,000 beauty fests for all ages take place annually. We've got everything from Little Miss Rural Electrification to Miss Scratch Ankle. Makes your heart race, doesn't it?

Three to four million women compete for crowns and scholarships every year. That's a lot of pulchritude (hopefully), and, all jokes aside for the moment, I'm not sure how I feel about such an emphasis on physical attributes.

Watching and cheering our favorite beauties on TV is a lot different from sitting near the runway in the auditorium. One judge was quoted as saying TV brushes up imperfections pretty well. Sitting up close and personal there in the auditorium though affords a not-so-satisfying view of warts and cellulite when the parading starts. Something about that strikes me as perverse.

But I don't know. If a girl looks darn good and wants to cash in on her assets, she has a right to go for the gold. Get that money and go to school, honey.

But as your next Ms. Mississippi Senior, maybe, I can tell you I will give the scholarship money to charity or get the pageant people to build me a hot tub. I'm too old to go back to school. The sponsors can forget that. No long-term goals for me.

As one contestant in the 1993 Ms. Senior Palm Beach County pageant told the master of ceremonies when he asked her about her life goals: "Honey," she said, "I don't even buy green bananas."

Well, that's all I've got to say about that. Got to go hunt up my white chiffon gown.

Birdwatchers Have More Fun

I was thinking about that Colorado mountain climber the other day—you know, the guy who was trapped by an eight hundred pound boulder and freed himself by sawing his own arm off with a dull pocket knife.

This is just way more than I can imagine. Or want to.

And this man smiles for the news cameras, adjusts his bandaged arm, and vows he's going to continue his solitary treks up and around rocky cliffs.

Pardon me while I unwrinkle my brow.

Don't misunderstand. I'm crazy about the great out-of-doors, but tippy toe-ing down a hot pier to the beach is about as uncomfortable as I'm willing to get.

Actually, I've become pretty doggone good lately at observing the great out-of-doors from my den couch—a sedentary pastime I should recommend to the mountain climber fellow because it certainly beats bleeding knuckles and severed arms.

My safe and pleasant couch pastime happened because, on a whim, I bought a sack of birdseed and set up two feeder pans on my patio. I can sit on the couch and watch the birds flock to feed.

Now, in and of itself, my feeding the birds is no great alliance with Mother Nature. It's spring. There's plenty of tasty stuff around for birds to eat. They could swoop down in almost anybody's yard and feast. But I bought that sack of birdseed and can't throw the bag away until it's empty.

So I fill the pans and they come. Big birds. Little birds. Blue jays. Sparrows. Black birds. Red birds. Pigeons.

And a squirrel.

The birds hate the squirrel—I know because they squawk like crazy when he comes around. They hate the squirrel because he trots up and promptly sits in the middle of the big pan and picks out all the sunflower seeds, which, I'm guessing, are the most delicious seeds in the lot.

Now I'll get to the exciting part.

The other day I was lounging on the couch with my morning coffee and newspaper. I'd put out the day's allotment of birdseed, and I could hear the birds chirping and singing, happy with their gourmet breakfast. But soon the chirping and singing turned to squawking, a signal that the pesky squirrel had arrived.

Then what to my wondering eyes did appear but the brilliant redbird (the male, I understand) at my bay window. He sat on the pane ledge and fluttered his wings against the glass, as if to tell me to get my boo-tay off that couch and come out there and chase Mr. Squirrel away.

Honest. So I did.

The next morning the same thing happened. And the next.

After the fourth day I was completely mesmerized by the redbird's behavior and found myself peering from behind my morning paper, hoping the squirrel would show up soon so the redbird and I could communicate.

When son Tom came for a visit I told him about this crazy scenario that was being repeated morning after morning with my bird friend, and Tom said, "I was sitting here in the den this morning before you got up and I saw exactly what you're saying. The redbird came to the window and fluttered his wings against the pane, and I looked out and saw a squirrel in the birdseed pan."

See? Tom is my witness. I'm not making this up.

A faithful reader had written me a fascinating letter about her bird watching hobby, and I have to admit that when I read her words I shrugged and thought, "Well, different strokes for different folks."

But now I understand her fascination. And the best part about this bird watching is that I'm enjoying nature without having to saw off my arm with a dull pocket knife.

I'm real glad about that.

Borin' Explorin' With Bebe

Is there anything elders won't do to humor grandchildren?

Take me, for instance. I've been entertaining Stanley Lambchop for a week, taking him with me everywhere, snapping his picture in interesting poses and places, making sure he has been properly introduced all around.

Unless you're a librarian or a kid, you probably don't recognize Stanley Lambchop's name. He's actually called "Flat Stanley" because he was supposedly beaned by an enormous bulletin board that fell from over his bed. He's flat as a pancake, small and laminated, and just the cutest little 6" posterboard fellow in his blue pants and orange shirt, his arms raised in a frozen greeting.

In his stories, Flat Stanley maintains that being squashed flat is not all that bad. He can be a kite or a placemat or just about anything where flatness is good. And flatness is very good if one must be mailed in an envelope to Bebe (that's me) for a visit.

Flat Stanley, you see, is the subject of a project being conducted by granddaughter Meredith's second grade class in Mobile. Class members have sent their "Flat Stanleys" all over creation, and when the Stanleys return (with pictures) a giant display of their travels and experiences will teach the children a lot about geography and regional culture.

Creative idea, huh? Yeah, but there was only one problem. Or two.

I didn't really have time for a house guest, and what in the world was I going to do with him?

First of all, I figured any little creature would love the farm, so I took Flat Stanley out to our barn. With a wad of chewing gum stuck to his back for support, he balanced on one of the horse stalls as Stoney the pony tried to nibble his right arm. Then I stuck him on the ladder going up to the hay loft. Every kid loves a hay loft.

He perched on the tractor, he climbed a tree, he dangled from the pasture fence—all while dutiful Bebe snapped his picture.

Then I took him to the park and let him swing and slide. A pretty teenager was there, so he cuddled in her lap. No wonder that smile is plastered on his face.

We went to the church and he lounged on the organ as I got music ready for Sunday services. He can't sing a note in a bucket, but I think he enjoyed the peace and quiet in the sanctuary, as I always do.

Next we paid a visit to the retirement home where he leaned on the piano as great-grandmother Edith played "Church in the Wildwood." He also had his picture made later with great-grandmother Marjorie, sitting in a golf cart, ready for a little sport or, at the least, a leisurely ride in this beautiful spring weather.

A day or two later I snapped Flat Stanley as he sat in the pink begonias beside a couple of Easter eggs. Experiencing a sudden burst of creativity, I added a ceramic Easter bunny to the scene. Eureka! Flat Stanley discovers the Easter Bunny. I figured this was about as exciting as it gets.

But then his Aunt Jamie showed up. Here was a photo op not to be missed as Jamie loves the camera. We opened hubby G-Man's grill, plopped down a roll of duct tape (the closest thing to a steak we had on hand), and placed Flat Stanley in the middle of the duct tape. As our little paper man waved wildly at the camera, Jamie, smiling broadly, barbecue fork in hand, pretended to be cooking him.

Yes, obviously, my wee guest had just about worn out his welcome.

Flat Stanley and his disposable camera pictures, quite the cultural documentary, are on their way back to Mobile as I write this. I'm sure his borin' explorin' week with Bebe will be extremely educational for Meredith and her classmates.

And whatcha bet I will not be asked to entertain his little flat boo-hiney ever again?

Brave Bikers Bestowed Bravos

"Avoiding crashes, suffering from
dehydration, driving to an epic
victory atop majestic Luz-Ardiden,
and finally riding 33+ mph in the
drenching rain all paid off as
Lance Armstrong and Team USPS
drove the 148 men left in the peloton
home to Paris."
— www.lancearmstrong.com

With brutally aching joints and muscles aflame, jerking and straining as the thin, hard wheels spun beneath him . . . the speeding biker centered the flag pole.

Perhaps you think I'm writing about Lance Armstrong, which I will, but to set the stage I had to take hubby G-Man back to his childhood and place him on his 1954 Schwinn Red Phantom, barreling across the school playground, reveling in the lead he maintained over a pal—until he hit the flag pole smack dab in the middle.

The ordeal, all the blood and angst, came back to G-Man as we watched Armstrong pedal his way to victory for the fifth straight year in the Tour de France a few weeks ago.

"Do you have any idea the pain those guys are going through?" G-Man asked as we grimaced in front of the TV. Biting the knuckle of my right index finger, I silently cheered Lance while (ukkk!) imagining the agony of enlarged lungs and boil encrusted buttocks from twenty-one straight days of cycling.

Of course, I knew. I mean, isn't everyone intrigued with self-flagellation and torture?

I was especially interested this year though because I read one of the funniest books ever last summer. The book, FRENCH REVOLUTIONS by British journalist Tim Moore, describes Moore's successful (but arduous) attempt to bike the Tour de France route prior to the "real thing" back in the summer of 2000.

As Moore explained at the beginning of the book, he thought he was simply embarking on a carefree bicycle cruise through rural French vineyards and sunflower fields. There was something about the Alps though that got his attention. But that was only after he'd spent agonizing days pushing those pedals hundreds of miles.

Moore wrote, "In the first seven days, [Tour de France] riders would cover a distance that in different and rather foolish circumstances would see them pedaling up to the outskirts of Warsaw."

But, ah, little G-Man on his '54 Schwinn could have given Moore and Armstrong a run for their money and the yellow jersey had his serious biking career not ended with the flagpole debacle.

Did G-Man sit and cry while blood streamed down his face and neck, his pale 10 year old visage turning into a ghastly mess? No, indeed.

"I got back on the bike and rode home," he bragged, shrugging. "What could I do? I didn't have a cellphone."

And there you have it. The spirit of a true biker. The courage. The perseverance. The incredible bladder busting determination to ride, whatever the price.

Anyway, at the height of the 2003 Tour de France, I stood there in front of that TV, frowning as I watched Lance Armstrong battle the German guy for the lead somewhere on a cobblestoned street lined with hundreds of screaming Europeans. I could only imagine that at that point the riders would all probably be happy as punch to pull over to a sidewalk cafe and have some croissants and raspberries with cream.

Beaning a flagpole is no fun, but telling about it later is, I guess, pretty fabulous. Just like the Tour de France. Those guys (believe-me-buddy!) can brag about taking themselves to the pits of physical annihilation—and living to tell the tale.

It's the biker spirit.

A favorite Tour de France story is about a competitor in 1967 named Tom Simpson. Unfortunately he crashed, and his last words (yep, LAST!) were, "Put me back on the bloody bike."

Not me, friend. I'm with Tim Moore who quipped, "As last words go, these are about as likely to pass my lips as 'It's time someone taught those ostriches a lesson.'"

I gave up my shiny blue Western Flyer in 1959 when Daddy gave me the keys to our old black Hudson. I've been styling ever since—with no blisters and no loss of blood.

But hurrah to the bikers. I'd give the world for their stamina—and their thighs (she says while biting into her croissant).

Viva la bicyclette!

Chilling Out With Miz Snippets

When I bought my dining room table several years ago, I was fascinated to learn the table had quite a history. An old English piece, this long oak table with sides that raise up and down is actually a cooling board.

Ever heard of such a thing?

Seems way back before funeral homes got to be so fancy, the dearly departed were simply laid out in state (prior to burial) in the home, sometimes in the living room and quite often in the dining room on these wake tables or cooling boards.

Our table is very old and probably served as a cooling board on many occasions.

Chilling thought, yes?

Well, that's why I mention it. The dining room table has nothing to do with anything, really. It's just that I've been wracking my brain, trying to drag forth every cool related item I can think of in order to come up with creative beat-the-heat suggestions for us Southern Fried Folks.

I'm not suggesting we climb around on the dining room table . . . or eat around it, for that matter. A cooling board is not for everybody, especially if somebody's got to die or I've got to cook.

Anyway, since other journalists are writing about the obvious heat battlers like air conditioners, iced tea, and wide brimmed bonnets, I want to give you the results of my divergent thinking on the subject.

Why go with boring solutions to this summertime heat when you can cool off more ingeniously?

*First of all, everybody should know about turning their pillows to the cool side. Wake up hot and sweaty during the night? Just flip your pillow over and there you go. Instant cool.

*Have some friendly florists in your parts? Tell them you'd like to browse in their refrigerated area.

I did that with my granddaughter a few weeks ago on her seventh birthday. We went to the flower shop so she could select seven flowers for a special birthday bouquet. Little did I know she'd go for expensive long-stemmed red roses and elegant spider lilies, but we spent a good forty-five minutes in that refrigerated room as she contemplated her selections.

The frigid air was worth every penny for posies.

*This hint is ages old, but it works: Lie down in a shady spot and cover your face with slices of cucumber. Scares the kids and dogs away too.

*Now, here's a novel idea. My sister Kathy told me a sales clerk swore to her that she always puts her underwear in the freezer about an hour before she dresses. Keeps her cool all day long, the clerk said.

Whoa now. I think that gal might be a bit numb somewhere farther up her body than her boo-tay . . . say, just about where her brains used to park. Brrrr.

*Moving right along, did you know there are such things as Cool Bandanas? Available in patterns ranging from Wild Safari to Jamaican Breeze, these kerchiefs are made of a special synthetic fabric advertised to "suck the heat right out of your body."

Wait a sec. Let's reign in a bit on all this creative stuff.

I can picture myself, decked out in my Jamaican Breeze bandana, cucumbers on my roseate cheeks, sporting icy britches and a lily in my clasped hands . . . stretched in cool comfort on the dining room table 'cause the doggone kerchief sucked all the heat right out of my body.

I 'spect I'll just flip my pillow to the cool side, thank you.

Column Trivia

Summer is the traditional time for family travel—the time to visit loved ones, gathering hugs and precious memories. And so it was that hubby G-Man and I decided, spur of the moment, to drive to Denver to see our son Tom and his lovely wife, Katie.

Driving to Denver is no walk in the park. We're talking 1200 miles plus. And we're also talking about scooting across an endless bit of real estate called Kansas. Ain't nothing there, folks. Yawwwwwn.

But there are some things most excellent about a long road trip.

First of all, I would, as usual, take notes on the trip and have plenty of trivia for a column. Second, there are no horses and no golf (yes!) to interrupt my quality time with G-Man. He would be a captive audience and I'd take advantage.

We set off, traveling up 61, listening to an Oldies station and singing along: "Get out in that kitchen and rattle those pots and pans! Shake, rattle, and roll..."

I interrupt G-Man's bass rumblings.

"Hey, see those wildflowers?" I say. "That's coreopsis."

He replies "uh huh," and even though I really have no idea if the yellow wildflowers are coreopsis, I do know that he sure as snuff doesn't have a clue. So I'm one up on him and we're not even out of Mississippi yet.

We travel on, pen and notebook in my lap. I'm flipping the radio to find more oldies or news, and hear on one country channel that Smokey the Bear was "born" in 1944. I was too, so this is exciting, scholarly lore. I write this Smokey history down.

We're barreling across the roadways of Arkansas and my attention is drawn to a sign announcing the exit to Toad Suck Park. When we stop for the night around Conway, I read in the hotel literature that Toad Suck Park got its name from whiskey drinkers years ago. "Them fellows drank so much whiskey, a-sucking on the bottle, that they went and blowed up like gigantic toads." I figure I can use this information somewhere, sometime. I record it.

The next day I try to get G-Man to join me in a game of license plate spotting. I like to look for wacky coded plates—like this one I spied somewhere on the Muskogee Turnpike: "IML8AGN."

Get it? No? Well, think about it.

That game fades fast because G-Man won't play, so I flip the radio some more. This was a good move because I hear a story about a big brother who had rigged up a bazooka-like gizmo that shot broccoli at his little brother to keep the kid out of Big Bro's bedroom.

I'm impressed and I jot it down.

We enter Kansas, where every QuikStop bears witness to their most famous celebrity couple—Dorothy and Toto. The little faces are everywhere: coffee mugs, key chains, bumper stickers, novelty toilet paper.

I take note.

After spending the night in Colby, Kansas, we head toward Denver. G-Man is talking on the cellphone much of the morning, so for a good while I'm alone with my thoughts and I scribble them in the notebook.

One in particular is troublesome. I think about this (as have so many before me): Can deer really read those yellow signs that tell them where to cross the highway?

Finally, we arrive. Big Denver. We're about to spend several days with Tom and Katie. We're dead tired, but a bunch of kisses and hugs would alleviate that.

They do, most effectively.

We do the whole laid-back city thing, sightseeing and eating in great restaurants—Greek, Italian, Mexican, and Ethiopian. We talk and laugh for hours. When the time comes to leave several days later, we cry. The trip has been worth every minute of travel.

Well, G-Man and I have returned, happy (a la Dorothy and Toto) to be home, but glad we decided to make that exhausting road trip.

Special moments with loved ones justify long hours on the road, no doubt about it.

And look here: I pull out my trusty notebook . . . and voila!

Such as it is, I've got a column.

Coming of Age With WLAC

Once upon a summertime, a season stashed a lifetime away in my memory but not so far away in my heart, a fellow named Gene Nobles came into my life.

I'd been out catching lightning bugs in a fruit jar, racing around and jumping ditches— a knobby kneed, thirteen year old girl with nothing better to do on a summer evening.

Truth is, at that time the only other pastime that could even come near the magic of pinching tails off lightning bugs (and watching the de-tailed appendage continue to flash on and off and on and off) was tadpole dipping. I'd probably been doing that too if we'd had some good rains, I can't recall, but I do remember the lightning bugs because I had the jar there by the radio on my nightstand when I first met Mr. Nobles.

Don't get me wrong. I wasn't a complete tomboy. I took great pride in the thirteen crinoline petticoats I could pull off in one swift swoosh, leaving them standing at attention in a single lacy stack in the corner of my bedroom. I did like pretty things. And romantic notions. And spinning 45 records on the hi fi or listening to folks like Bill Haley, Teresa Brewer, and Dean Martin on my RCA AM radio.

Piccolino flats were lined up in my closet—red, black, green, yellow—just waiting for junior high in the fall. Yes indeed, I knew thrilling moments were in the near future, glittering on the horizon like the tails of a thousand lightning bugs.

Every summer evening I'd sit on the side of the bathtub and wash my grotty feet, which is probably what I was doing that night when my friend Delia called.

"Turn the radio on at 10:15," she said. "You may have to set it in the window and twist it around some, but put it on 1510. That's the station that girl at the Keene Freeze told us about . . ."

So through that evening, in cotton jammies, and with lightning bugs and scrubbed feet, I sat on my rumpled bed and listened to the requests on Pete Webb's local radio show, "Pete's Platter Party," until 10:15 — then tuned the dial to 1510 and fell in love with . . . Gene Nobles.

Introduced by "Swannee River Boogie," the voice of Nobles swept into my bedroom and that of millions of teenagers throughout twenty-eight states on mega watts of glorious music from WLAC, Nashville's premier radio station. Sponsored by Randy's Record Shop in Gallatin, Tennessee—at that time the largest mail-order phonograph record shop in all creation—Nobles beamed us rhythm and blues, rock and roll, and sometimes a bit of gospel, and we loved every soulful minute of it.

Goodbye, Pat Boone, Perry Como, Patti Page. Hey, goodbye to Bill Haley and his square, jellyroll-haired Comets as well.

We were in Coolsville now, rockin' to the real thing—Fats Domino ("Yes, it's me and I'm in love again . . ."), Bo Diddley, Jerry Lee Lewis, Jimmy Reed, Little Richard ("Tutti frutti, allll rootie!"), Chuck Berry ("Oh, Mabellene, why cancha be truuuuue? You done started back doin' the things you usta do!")—and dreaming about our one true love as we swooned to the mellow notes of the Platters ("Oh-oh-oh, yes, I'm the great pretender . . ."), and, of course, Elvis, whose "I want you, I need you, I love you" set many a teenage heart afire.

I doubt I ever chased any more lightning bugs. Didn't need to. I had the pure magic of Gene Nobles coming from my little radio that summer night and many, many nights thereafter.

Life was sparkling . . . and I was heading for junior high.

Country Mouse Offers Tribute to NYC

This country mouse crept into New York City several months ago. Hubby G-Man had business there, and I had plans to visit with three friends—former Mississippian Bruce Levingston, concert pianist of renown, and two writer pals, Carol Skolnick and Bob Civin.

New York City may as well be Mars to my provincial mind, so after seeing G-Man off for the day I dressed and headed for Greenwich Village—two hours early for my luncheon date with Carol. Wanted to be sure I'd be on time.

I left the hotel, flagged a taxi, asked the driver to take me to an Indian restaurant, Mirchi, at 29 7th Avenue, and settled back to congratulate myself on being brave enough to tackle this mind boggling city on my own. New York taxi drivers are wonderful, but they have to be among the most aggressive drivers on the face of the earth. I didn't do much settling, just gripped the seat with white knuckles and prayed.

Safely arriving at the restaurant, I paid the driver and turned around to find the place locked tight—a sign said Mirchi wouldn't open for another hour. I'd planned to sit quietly in a booth with my book and a cup of coffee. Carol wasn't to arrive for over an hour.

What should I do? I had no idea where I was or what the neighborhood was like or what I'd do if somebody grabbed me or how tightly I should hold my purse or which direction to go for a walk or if I took off from that very spot I'd be able to find my way back or . . . I was a mess.

I knew I couldn't just stand there on the corner. Bumpkin, I may be, most definitely lacking a fallen sisterhood aura, still I knew standing on a city street corner would not be a good idea.

After a minute or two of deep and painful thought, I decided to walk straight south on 7th. I wrapped my purse straps around my neck, put my nerve endings on alert for muggers, took a deep breath, and headed down the street.

After walking for blocks, I (eureka!) spotted an open deli. Alleluia, gulps and more gulps. My life was saved.

Entering the deli, I found a table by the window, ordered coffee, and opened my book. I wondered if the other people there could tell I was a "foreigner."

Poor folks, I thought. They're stuck in this big old crowded city with squashed lives and spirits. What an empty existence they have, never speaking to others and keeping to themselves. They don't know what they're missing not living in my wonderful rural area of the Deep South where folks are friendly and helpful.

Rather than read, I began to look out the deli's big front window. I saw bikes and parking meters. Not a building less than ten stories. Pigeons and sidewalk vents. Taxis, vans, buses, New Jersey trucks. Skinny young girls with long hair and funky clothes. Backpacks. Perky caps. Teenage boys in baggy jeans. Old women pushing shopping carts. Delivery guys and more delivery guys. Jay-walkers. Earphones and cellphones. Canes. More vans. More delivery trucks. McDonald sacks. Dreadlocks and windbreakers. Berets. A guy in a Tulane cap.

A Tulane cap? Wait a sec. What's this southern soul doing up here in no man's land? No sane persons—well, except for my friends Bruce, Carol, and Bob—could live in a place like this. Could they?

An empty table sat between me and a lone woman about my age. Dressed in khaki pants, sneakers, and a light jacket, the woman looked as if she could have just popped in from a leisurely Saturday morning stroll here on Mississippi soil or a run to the corner grocery. She leaned her curly blond head toward me.

"Excuse me," she said. "When you ordered your coffee I detected a southern accent. Are you visiting our city?"

Then, would you believe? We started to chat. Her name was Nelda. She had lived in New York City thirty years and loved it. She worked as a researcher for an author. She spoke with a distinct New York accent . . . and she was delightful.

The next half hour passed in fine fashion, and when it was time to go she walked with me part of the five or six blocks back to Mirchi so I wouldn't get lost.

Since the September 11 attacks I think often about Bruce, Carol, Bob, all the Neldas, the baggy britches teenagers, the old women pushing their little bags of groceries home in shopping carts. New York City is not some dungeon of aloof, inhospitable people, but a beautiful city of spectacular diversity—dreadlocks, berets, Tulane caps. And they're not lacking in friendliness or compassion for obviously misplaced persons like me.

I'm pulling for 'em.

Diary of a Mad Strutter

MONDAY, MARCH 3: I've lost my mind. In a weak moment, I agreed to march in the St. Paddy's Day parade in Jackson with the "Struttin' Strumpets," a group of girls with questionable Millsaps College diplomas (circa late'60s) who are feverishly grasping in their old age for a few more wild and crazy days.

My cousin Marg roped me into this. She and the others are a tad younger than I, and are not new to wild and crazy. I am. They thought I'd never accept, but I fooled 'em. Besides, all the proceeds go to the Blair E. Batson Hospital for Children—one of my favorite charities. I'm so excited I can't stand it.

TUESDAY, MARCH 4: Marg said I should get my costume ordered ASAP because the other tramps in the parade might wipe out our inventory. Already did that—ordered yesterday afternoon. The Strumpets all dress alike. Purple flapper dresses with miles of fringe. Towering purple wigs. Black (and wicked) fishnet stockings. White turkey feather boas. Absurdity, insanity, and strict uniformity are the rules. The motto is something altogether different, and that's all I'll say about that.

WEDNESDAY, MARCH 5: The costume arrived before noon today. Of course, I had to try it on immediately. My friend Daisy said, "Oooh, girl, you look good in that short purple dress with yo' big legs." Gave me pause.

I will have to remember to scooch in behind some of the other Strumpets when pictures are made so all of me is not front and center. Marg says the Strumpets are the most photographed group in the parade other than the Sweet Potato Queens, but with my addition this year she's sure we might surpass them. I most definitely can strike a pose. I've been practicing.

THURSDAY, MARCH 6: The Strumpets want hubby G-Man to be a cabana boy, pulling the water wagon or carrying the boom box. Marg says she has a green leprechaun hat he can wear. They're also planning to order purple pants and attractive painted muscle body shirts with "Struttin' Strumpets Staff" on the back. He's balking.

FRIDAY, MARCH 7: Received word this morning that we Strumpets will meet on Saturday morning before the parade to rehearse our dance routine. The music of choice is "Louie, Louie," and I have an idea my one bit of hoofin' skills (Shuffle/Ball/Step) will not fit into the moves they're planning.

SATURDAY, MARCH 8: Modeled my purple costume for the grandkids, who squealed with delight. I think I remind them of Barney.

SUNDAY, MARCH 9: G-Man is still balking. Marg says if he'd just put on the stupid outfit and some big sunglasses, nobody will know who he is. When the throngs begin screaming at him because he looks so cool—and because they want "Beads, Mister!"—he'll be transported into the euphoria of the whole wacky affair. He's saying something about decorum, and I'm saying, "Decorum, schmorum. You don't get an opportunity like this every day." If you ask me, I believe the problem is the leprechaun hat.

MONDAY, MARCH 10: My poor treadmill doesn't understand all this activity. I'm going at it twice a day, which has put blisters on both heels and nagging aches in assorted places. At least I don't have to worry about my spider veins because the fishnet stockings provide sufficient camouflage. The girls planned well there.

TUESDAY, MARCH 11: This morning I put "Louie, Louie" on the CD player and gyrated up and down the hall. I never have had a problem with rhythm, it's just that simultaneously moving/breathing is more difficult now than it used to be. We're to dance for two minutes in front of the judges' stand at the Governor's Mansion. Marg says I shouldn't worry—the cabana boys will have wet cloths and smelling salts.

Chances are good hubby G-Man will continue to refuse to be a lowly cabana boy. In my opinion, the silly man just needs to grow up.

WEDNESDAY, MARCH 12: No time [*puff*] to write [*puff, puff*] any more about this [puff] till after the parade. Have to stay on [*puff*] this treadmill [*puffffff*]...

~~~~~~

Addendum — The 2003 parade, all 600 miles of it (or so it seemed), is over. My spray-on tan is fast fading. My purple nail polish is chipped. Purple eye liner and stick-on tattoo are long gone. I'm but a shadow of my Struttin' Strumpet self, but there's joy in my heart.

For one solid weekend I was a rootin' tootin' middle-aged queen. I won't soon forget it

The Divine Secrets of the Fantabulous ELDs

With all the new grandbabies hubby G-Man and I have acquired during the past five months, I've found myself doing lots of interesting things—like going to bunches of movies, not with the babies, but with the older grandchildren, keeping them entertained and out of Mama's and Daddy's played out presence.

I'll be honest. Sitting in a cool, dark theater, munching popcorn and guzzling icy soft drinks, escaping diapers and bottles, was worth every excruciating Bam! and Wham! of the interminably long and scary *SPIDERMAN* film. I also sat through *JIMMY NEUTRON: BOY GENIUS* as well as *THE ROOKIE*, the new *E.T.* and several others equally as hypnotic.

I do love movies, but I have to light a stick of dynamite under G-Man to get him out of his recliner so he can go snooze in the theater. No lie, the man slept through *ROCKY*, which was probably the last movie we saw together.

I have, therefore, grabbed every opportunity to plan these "educational field trips" to the movies with the little ones. Cartoons to spiders, I don't care. Just throw me the Milk Duds and leave me alone.

One brand spanking new movie I was determined to make (without the kids—the film is PG-13) was *THE DIVINE SECRETS OF THE YA YA SISTERHOOD*, based on the book by Rebecca Wells. First chance I got, I went.

After seeing the Ya Ya gals in all their glory on the big screen, I became most nostalgic for my very own juvenile sisterhood, and so (may I have a drum roll?) I am now about to spill some bodacious beans.

Please understand that I type this with great reverence: My playmates and I were the nine year old wicked belles of the ELDs.

Never heard of the ELDs? Well, of course not, we kept things hush hush.

Nobody was to know the meaning of ELD, except us girls, and we had the most wonderful meetings once a week after school at a member's home. Our mamas cooperated by supplying us with lots of chips and drinks, and on one special occasion we had real food—banana splits.

I can't remember anything we really did other than eat, but every now and then I'm sure we conducted business.

In fact, fifty years after the organization of the ELDs, I will now share the only piece of business I can recall, which also necessitates my revealing [gasp] the meaning of our name, ELD.

There were eight of us third graders. At our initial meeting we tossed around exotic names we could call our club, eventually settling on (aggggh!) Eight Little Devils.

Eight Little Devils we were for several weeks as we ate our way through bag after bag of potato chips, but one day we were forced to put the chips down and confront a very important issue.

Several of the members wanted to invite another girl to join our club.

Well, hold on. If we invited a new member, there would be nine Eight Little Devils, which anybody can see does not compute. Hence we commenced another business meeting.

What should we do?

Standing before the sisters in Patricia Baskin's backyard, I announced that I had the perfect solution. We could stay ELDs forever and ever. All we had to do was change the meaning of ELD—sort of a sacrilege, but a lot better than trying to come up with another name with the same punch.

Nobody objected because we were all anxious to get over to our friend's house and thrill her with our exclusive membership invitation.

The vote was unanimous, and the Eight Little Devils quickly became the...Evil Ladies of the Dark.

Afterwards, we stood in a circle, spit on the ground, and that was that.

Hey, if Hollywood wants the ELD story for another blockbuster of a movie I'll be delighted to dig back into my fading memory and blab more.

I wouldn't tell all this, but I figure, sad to say, after fifty years the statute of limitations is bound to have expired on the E-xquisite, L-uscious, D-ivine secrets of the plucky, pig-tailed Evil Ladies of the Dark.

Doughnut Dolly In Vietnam

This story is about treasure in my attic and about one gutsy gal—my sister Kathy, eighteen months my junior and my best buddy in many shenanigans. Kathy was always one to jump into the thick of things. Caution? What's that?

After coaching high school girls' basketball and winning one game, maybe two, the entire 1966-67 season, Kathy got a hankering to join the Red Cross and see the world—Vietnam, to be specific.

We were horrified. Mother cried. Daddy paced the floor. But the girl was determined. She went to New York for training, then flew off to join the war.

The stack of letters and twenty-five reel-to-reel tapes Kathy sent home from Vietnam that year have been languishing in a trunk in my attic. I thought about her letters and tapes the other day after I'd waved my brother Bill off for his new adventure--a year teaching conversational English in Korea.

After telling Bill goodbye, my mind turned to Kathy's leaving home for Viet Nam so many years ago. I decided to look for her letters.

Braving the dusty clutter in my attic, I found the old trunk and retrieved her correspondence, then sat and read.

To see the Vietnam War through Kathy's eyes is fascinating. I'll have to wait to listen to the tapes. They'll have to be changed from reel-to-reel to some more modern medium, but I chuckle as I recall listening in 1968 to one of her taped comments. I remember she was chatting away, sitting in her little trailer, telling us something like this:

"Tonight is Tet, and the Vietnamese are really celebrating. Fireworks are going off all over the place. Shouting. Hollering. If I didn't know better, I'd think they were right here in the compound . . ." [Remember the 1968 Tet Offensive when the Viet Cong slipped into the military compounds? Fireworks nothing! Whole lot of shooting going on that night.]

In her letters, Kathy talks of being stationed in Pleiku, in Long Binh, and in Qui Nhon. The Doughnut Dollies (so-called because they gave the guys doughnuts, coffee, and lots of cheer) ran rec centers on bases or went out in clubmobile units, traveling around the countryside every day. They flew in choppers, and rode in jeeps, trucks and tanks. They flew out to the smaller fire bases where they programmed to the different artillery units, engineers, and special forces.

Kathy wrote: "To see the expression on the faces of the men out in the boonies who haven't seen an American girl in four or five months is an experience. I sat down to a c-ration lunch with some of these guys yesterday and they almost couldn't talk to me. One guy said, 'Lady, I don't mean to stare, but you're the first girl I've seen in four months, and I really don't know how to act.' In a way it seemed funny, but actually it was sad. The majority of them look too young to be away from home, much less [to be] fighting a war."

Kathy was twenty-two, too young to be in the midst of war as well.

"So far I've only been in one mortar attack and one ground attack," she wrote. "I can't imagine how the guys feel out there in the field as they face this danger constantly. We're talking about facing death every day."

What a treasure our family has in this box of correspondence from the past, thanks to Kathy Boswell Nichols.

And as for brother Bill, modern technology will facilitate our messaging. Instant e-mail will deliver news and pictures of his daily goings-on in Korea during the next twelve months—a wonderful thing when beloved family is far away.

Progress is marvelous; I will treasure every electronic message from Bill. But after losing myself in Kathy's yellowed letters from Viet Nam, I can't help but wish e-mail could arrive with a smudge, a crinkle, and yes, one teeny tiny tear stain or two.

Eating Dirt

"If a lump of soot falls into the soup
and you cannot conveniently get it out,
stir it in well and it will give the soup
a French taste." — Jonathan Swift

I'm going to get down and dirty here, so don't keep reading if you're averse to such things. I also recommend your not continuing to read if you're snacking, especially while chewing on something straight from the garden.

And why?

Because the latest info from the American Dietetic Association tells us that, like it or not, each of us probably eats several pounds of dirt from birth to death, and no matter how well we wash those turnip greens or carrots we're still going to be putting down some reechy matter.

Since it's time to start hauling in veggies from our gardens, I thought I ought to alert everybody to this new information, although the old saying "You've got to eat a peck of dirt before you die" has been around for generations. Anybody with a baby has quoted that one.

The U. S. Food and Drug Administration says it's really impossible to get all the dirt and foreign objects (insects, rodent hairs, worms, maggots!) off our food, fresh and processed, but for the most part, the USFDA states, this unappetizing stuff won't kill us or even make us sick.

That's good to know.

I still have fond childhood memories of pulling radishes straight from the garden, washing those suckers off with the hose, and eating 'em like candy. Makes my mouth water to think about it. Little did I know I was digesting a palatable portion of grit and grime also, no matter how long I washed those radishes.

And as little bitties, sister Kathy and I had the most adorable playhouse where we spent hours making mudpies and cinnamon "coffee" in dusty bowls and cups. We never partook of our gourmet offerings but fed them instead to baby cousins and dogs. Must not have adversely affected them because they're still around. (Not the dogs — but the cousins seem all right.)

Then there are folks who eat dirt on purpose. You read that right. They're called geophages (from the Greek "geo"—earth and "phagein"—eat).

Trying to explain the attraction of soil gobbling, scientists and sociologists have come up with a bunch of explanations ranging from hunger to cravings to heredity. But when they ask geophages why they eat dirt, the main response is that dirt tastes good.

Well. I guess so.

One dirt eater in an article written by Associated Press writer Kathy Eyre compared her habit to using a pinch of chewing tobacco every day. Just about as healthy, I suppose.

Another lady claims she eats a cupful every afternoon while she watches TV and works her crossword puzzle. I can hear the conversation now: "Hey, honey, while you're up would you get me a cup of dirt?"

Dr. Kevin Grigsby, a social worker and professor of psychiatry and health behavior at Medical College of Georgia explains that geophagia exists all over the world and has for centuries, but is especially prevalent in the American South. That's a lot of dirt excavating.

No wonder we need kudzu for soil conservation.

Anyway, I was telling hubby G-Man about all this dirt eating research I was doing, and he said he didn't eat much dirt as a child, but did enjoy munching on chicken feed, the closest thing to junk food his mama kept around the house. He swears the little chicken feed pellets were tasty. (And this is a man who won't eat English peas.)

But listen, I've always maintained "to each his own." I'm not one to get all up into peoples' business. They can just proceed if they want to devour stuff like chicken feed and dirt (which, by the way, comes from the Old Norse word "drit," meaning excrement).

Not me. I'll dish the dirt, but there will be nary a time I'll intentionally eat it.

Elvis 101

"Elvis [was] the greatest cultural force in
the twentieth century. He introduced the beat
to everything, music, language, clothes—a
whole new social revolution."
                                    — Leonard Bernstein

Grandparents with panache aplenty understand that it is no longer enough to teach the little ones to bake sugar cookies, hook a bream, or play "Baby Bye" on the piano.

No, in today's dizzying world, we elders have the huge responsibility of making sure our grandchildren are exposed to activities that will enrich their lives forever.

That's why I found myself at Graceland in Memphis last week with Meredith, my eight year old granddaughter.

We were making memories for her to take home and store away for the day when she'd tell her own granddaughter, "Listen, kid, my grandmother gave me all sorts of educational opportunities . . ."

On the blistering, ninety degree day we made our pilgrimage, Meredith and I were two among many—I'm talking lots and lots and lots of humanity with throw-away cameras.

So, we were sitting on a bench at the grandiose Graceland Tourist Center, home of one hundred rockin' souvenir shops, watching throngs of Elvis Presley fans stuff themselves with mustard soaked hot dogs as they shuffled along in endless lines to catch the shuttle to the mansion.

We'd already inched through the *Lisa Marie* (Elvis's airplane), admiring the 24 karat gold-plated lavatories and plastic covered couches. We'd bumped our way through the crowded "King of Rock 'n Roll" museum that leads (surprise!) into yet another glittering souvenir shop.

We'd enjoyed the coolness of the darkened motorcycle and car display where Meredith oohed and sighed over the pink striped jeep and I gazed longingly at the Rolls.

We'd swayed to "Are You Lonesome Tonight?" and bounced our boo-tays to "Hound Dog" as we strolled the shopping mall.

We were Elvis saturated and satiated.

So anyway, we'd collapsed there on a bench outside one of the souvenir shops, and Meredith said, groaning, "Bebe, I think I don't want any more Elvis."

I was happy to hear it. Hot as a tater, my hunka hunka burnin' flesh was anxious to head south.

But now Meredith could go home with pictures (Boy, did we snap!) and she could impress friends with her newly acquired knowledge.

On the way home, she stuck a piece of Berry Splash Kooler gum in her mouth and, in between chews, said, "Bebe, I didn't know . . . Elvis was . . . so important."

Here was my chance to give the child an added dose of Rock 'n' Roll 101.

"Honey," I said, "Elvis Presley completely changed the world of popular music."

Predictably, she said, "Huh?" and I took that as an opportunity to lecture further.

"Yeah, listen," I said, "Elvis sold over one billion records worldwide, more than anyone in record industry history. He had gold and platinum records and fourteen Grammy nominations. Say 'Elvis' anywhere in the world and folks know who you're talking about."

She yawned, and I decided I needed to dig down for something more impressive.

"You know what?" I said to my smart, red-headed granddaughter. "When Elvis appeared on the Ed Sullivan show in January of 1957, a bunch of my friends came to my house to watch him. This was a big deal. It's unbelievable now, but the Sullivan directors would only show Elvis from the waist up because they said he shook his hips too much when he sang. Historians say this was one of television history's most memorable moments. And I saw it!"

She asked, "So Elvis could have been president?"

Yep, I knew my history lesson was sinking in.

"Maybe," I said. "I mean, this man's been dead since 1977, and over 600,000 folks still visit Graceland every year. Amazing."

I'm really impressing her now, I thought. This is information she'll remember always. A cultural bonanza.

About that time the car cell phone rang. It was her mother.

"Meredith," I whispered as she began to chat, "tell Mama what you learned today."

"Guess what, Mama!" she said, "You're not going to believe this . . . Elvis died on the potty!"

I blinked. Guess there are just some historical facts more impressive than others.

Explaining The Harley Zoom Zoom Syndrome

Surprise! Surprise! There's a new research study out (isn't there always?) about men and their primitive predisposition to things wacko—like dangerous sorts of things.

The newspaper report of this new study grabbed my attention because every now and then hubby G-Man argues with me about his desire for a Harley. He says yes; I say no.

So far my sensible thinking has prevailed, but after every motorcycle discussion I can't help but wonder why men are so dadgum stubborn and brash.

There's a television show called "Outdoor Sports" (on ESPN, I think), and last week I happened to catch several of the program's athletic events as I visited with friends. In one of the featured segments, the testosterone charged males were hacking at tall tree trunks with razor-sharp axes, stuffing a flat board in the indentation, climbing up on the flimsy board, hacking out another hole in the trunk, stuffing the board in the next hole, climbing still higher and higher—until they could, with grim determination, whack the top of the tree smack off.

My pal Bonnie turned to me and said, "Why do men do things like that?"

Her question was rhetorical; she knew I didn't have a clue.

Cruising along in my vehicular air conditioning the next day, I passed a fellow in the middle of nowhere. The guy peddled his bicycle down the highway under a brutal noon-day sun, his every muscle straining for one more push, one more push.

Obviously hot as blazes, hunkered over the bike's handlebars, this madman with set jaw was proving to all the passing world that, by golly, he was going to ride that bicycle until the tires fell off—assuming the rubber was shed before his scorched hide.

Men. Who can figure?

Why do they stubbornly pursue activities that are not only uncomfortable,

SNIPPETS

but also life threatening?

Well, the new research study says our answer lies in the male and female brains. There's a primitive, fundamental difference. Would you believe women's brains are better organized to perceive and remember emotional moments?

I'm talking about emotional moments as in, "Oh, yikers! I almost broke my neck climbing up that tree and I've figured out right fast that trees are for squirrels, not humans, and hereafter I will not clamber up tall tree trunks."

Or, "I rode my bike over to Betsy's house right after lunch and I was sweating bullets and almost had a heatstroke and that wasn't one bit fun and I will never ever in a million years do that again."

Males can't remember stuff like that.

This male/female brain research was reported in the Proceedings of the National Academy of Sciences (sounds impressive to me) by scholars who used all kinds of MRIs and neurological tests on a couple dozen subjects.

"The wiring of emotional experience and the coding of that experience into memory is much more tightly integrated in women than in men," the project director, Dr. Turhan Canli, stated in the NAS journal.

In laymen's terms, these results simply indicate women are less likely to splatter their brains and more likely to . . . think.

So there you go. Men are stubborn and brash because they can't remember squat.

Figures.

But don't go fussing at men about their brains or lack of. They'll just seize on that part of the research study that mentions emotional wiring. Women are too high-strung, they'll say. Too tightly wound.

Yeah, but we're not climbing trees with axes or speeding down the highway with bugs in our front teeth.

Ummm, did somebody mention "primitive"?

Furry Pharaoh

Since we're celebrating "Adopt-A-Pound-Puppy" month, I decided this is the perfect time to write about my new puppy Pharaoh and encourage folks to go to the closest animal shelter to rescue one of these precious creatures.

I've put off penning a column about Pharaoh for over a month. I guess I just didn't want to brag about how I have, without question, the finest dog anywhere around.

Yep, in spite of a bad habit or two, he's a most excellent fellow.

Hubby G-Man gave in to the pouting from grandson Wayne and me, stipulating that, OK, we could adopt Pharaoh from Wayne's litter of mixed breed pups, but this Heinz-57 would have to be a barn dog, and that was that.

And that WAS that for, oh, just long enough to get poochie from Wayne's house in south Mississippi up to these more northern reaches of the state. Then I put on the big sulk and whined to G-Man that nobody in his right mind could banish a little puppy to the mosquitoes and heat out at the barn.

G-Man capitulated quickly. He'd fallen in love with Pharaoh too.

So here we are with this beautiful black/brown/gray animal who grows bigger and bigger and bigger as the days go by. He's about four months old, weighs forty pounds, and his paws are as big as my face.

He has a ruff of white under his neck which looks for all the world like an ascot, giving him quite an aristocratic air, regal maybe—as a pharaoh should look, I guess.

And "Pharaoh"? Not your everyday name for a canine, huh?

That was Wayne's creation. Five year old Wayne is all into Egypt and pyramids, so the name "Pharaoh" was a natural selection.

I must say this name suits our Pha-Pha, for he's already the ruler of the house.

He has more toys than my grandchildren, and also has his own rolling, four drawer cart that holds extra food, chewy bones, snacks, fido cologne and brush.

And, of course, he is the happy possessor of a soft, cushiony bed and a special, bone shaped tray for his food and water dishes.

This dog is cruising.

How do we explain our adoration? Anybody who sits and strokes a pup's head and looks deep into his big brown doggie eyes can vouch for the spiritual connection between human and canine. It's there.

And I can see all over his little furball of a self that he wants to please me. He's learned to sit and fetch, he's house trained, and he now strolls happily on a leash with only the mildest of jerks and jolts.

However, deciding I needed a little more advanced help training Pharaoh with certain oral fixations (gnaw-gnaw-gnawww!), I went to town and bought an enlightening book titled "The Art of Raising a Puppy" by the Monks of New Skete. I was drawn to this book as soon as I saw it on the shelf because the dog on the cover is a dead ringer for Pharaoh.

The cover dog is a full-blooded German Shepherd—which convinced me that even though my Pha-Pha is a mixed breed, he obviously got all the right genes. People pay big bucks for the full blooded variety, and I get the same thing free in my pound pup. As friend Sandi said, "Who says God doesn't have a sense of humor!"

Anyway, I've been reading this book by these monks who live in upper New York state. They raise German Shepherds and they are canine savvy.

The monks stress the importance of "inseeing" on the part of the trainer.

"Inseeing is standing inside your dog's psyche, putting yourself at his center . . . and understanding him from that perspective," they write.

That's all well and good, but I had to write the monks with a very important question.

> Dear Monks of New Skete,
> My dog Pharaoh has a bad habit which is obviously
> meaningful to him. I don't want to mess up any
> kind of delicate psychological balance between
> the two of us, but I'm just wondering if in order to
> mesh with Pharaoh's psyche I have to chew up
> G-Man's sandals.
>
> Ptttuuie! Answer fast.
>
> Your friend,
> Beth

Getting My Get-Up-And-Go To Go With My Get-Up

My cowboy husband G-Man is a Mega-Type-A personality. I mean, he is the Type-A prototype—the blueprint, the model, the original "thang." He can't lounge, chill, or rest his bones. That's just not in his little book on How To Conquer The World. He's a man on the go.

Constantly.

He has always badgered me to be on the go with him. To encourage me, he bought me things. Cowgirl things. Do I have fringe? My dears, I have more fringe than a Victorian lampshade. Enough fringe makes you a cowgirl, right?

Wrong. Fringe phooey.

G-Man bought fringed leather jackets for me. He bought long, Marlboro-looking canvas coats with fringe. He bought cowgirl shirts with lacy fringe and cowgirl hats with fringy-looking, feathery headbands.

None of it worked.

The horses didn't understand this fringe made me a cowgirl. I'm sure they thought I was just some chicken-livered woman with shaky things on her bod. (I'm talking about the fringe, buster.)

We had a horse once that I could ride without getting nauseated. His name was Rex, and he was the King of the Out-to-Pasture Equines (KOPE). He was gentle and sweet. If I tugged on the reins, he'd stand there for a few seconds, giving me time to change my mind or figure out if the direction I tugged was really the direction I wanted to go. If I said, "Oh, helllllllp," he'd stop dead in his tracks. A real sweetheart, that animal.

Well, just when I was getting used to Rex and my bottom was growing accustomed to extended rides, G-Man decided to sell this gentleman horse and buy a steed for me that was a little more spirited.

Nosirree. I was having none of it.

This is where the hub and I parted extracurricular ways. I was tired of trying to keep up with him in the great outdoors.

G-Man sold Rex and bought Bandit, and I haven't climbed in the saddle since.

But I just couldn't stand to see that marvelous wardrobe go to waste. I now have the loveliest den curtains you've ever seen. Whipped them up myself. Western-looking fabric with leather trim, and—you got it—more fringe than a Texas bordello.

Frankly, I think the fringe belongs right there.

There's no question that compared to the back of a horse, my recliner is a much nicer spot to giddy-up.

Gettin My Mojo Workin'

"If I had to tell somebody who had never been
to the South, who had never heard of soul music,
what it was, I'd just have to tell him that it's music
from the heart, from the pulse, from the innermost
feeling. That's my soul, that's how I sing. And that's
the South." — Al Green

Back when I was no bigger than a tadpole, I enjoyed lounging with my buddies on the pink chenille bedspread of our friend, Stella Roberts, who had her own apartment behind the "big house" of Margaret and Dean Pearman in our quiet Mississippi Delta town.

This was a black-white situation, you see, back in the early '50s. Stella was the maid, and we little white neighborhood girls were her loyal subjects. We adored her, and she ruled the roost in this segregated corner of the universe.

Ahhh, did Stella ever rule.

Kathy, Judy, and I sprawled on her bed, stringing beads and eating soda crackers, listening to blues and barrelhouse music on the radio while Stella danced around the tiny, bare room, throwing her head back, waving her arms, moving her hips.

We'd watch and question her.

"Stella, how come you don't like Perry Como? Or Dinah Shore? How come you like music like that?"

She'd laugh big and say, "Girls, one day you find out what REAL music is. One day you find out what moves your soul."

The next thing we knew our mamas were preaching to us: "Y'all can't go hang out at Stella's any more on Saturday afternoons. You don't need to be listening to that trashy music."

Then we gave Judy a heap of hassle because she told her daddy about some of the words—mighty mild lyrics compared with what's out there today, for sure. Those lyrics didn't mean squat to three elementary school girls, because at that point we didn't know a thing about being love-sick or having powerful ways. Fact is, we weren't too knowledgeable about much of anything.

Well, we did know a couple of things.

We knew Stella could sure get down with the dancing, and we knew we kids were happy as pine borers in a fresh log when we were in her magical presence.

The really big thing we didn't realize as we hung out with Stella and her wonderful music was that we were hearing the birth, right then, of REAL Rock and Roll. Two years later, Mississippi born Elvis Presley combined blues and gospel, and there you have it.

Stella wasn't around the neighborhood two years later though. She went off and left us. Headed up Highway 61 with her one little bag of possessions, moving to Chicago, hoping to find a better life.

But as Kathy, Judy, and I entered our teenage years, we never forgot her.

Thanks to Stella, we three took a back seat to none on the dance floor. We were the sock hop queens (at least, in our opinion) because of our training on the polished hardwood of Stella's tiny one room quarters.

Stella was the best.

She put our mojos in high gear early on and taught us, yes indeed, what truly moves a young girl's soul.

Give My Regards To Broadway

At a seminar several years ago, Dr. David Potter, former Delta State University president, made this statement: "We each have the capacity to live many lives, but we end up living only one." His comment made me stop and think about the paths I've taken. I was reminded of a remote path, a most exotic path, for which I, the prototypical small-town girl, once yearned.

Didn't we all nurse some pretty wild dreams as youngsters?

Well, I'm confessing that as a child I was determined to have a career on Broadway. No Bette Midler was I, but music was my passion. My sister Kathy and I sang everywhere as preschoolers (whether people wanted to hear us or not). *"Dear Hearts and Gentle People," "Chattanooga Shoe Shine Boy," "O, You Beautiful Doll," "Mairzy Doats."* Name a song from the '40s or early '50s, and we sang it in little community shows, at parties, in front of restless captive cousins at family reunions.

A plain little girl, I stood for hours before my dressing table mirror, and, accompanied by my record player, I tossed my pigtails and sang my heart out. Sigmund Romberg's *"It"* and *"I Love To Go Swimmin With Wimmen,"* the Rogers and Hammerstein songs from *"South Pacific"* and *"Oklahoma,"* tunes from *"Kismet"* and *"Showboat."*

Ahhh! The stage. I couldn't wait to get to the big lights. My family endured the racket and patiently gave me privacy as I bellowed from my bedroom.

By the time I was in high school I was participating in summer theater at the University of Southern Mississippi. We performed Gilbert and Sullivan's *"Gondoliers,"* then *"Paint Your Wagon."* I was hooked.

During my undergraduate years at Millsaps College, I toured France/Germany for the USO and had a romp as Molly in *"The Unsinkable Molly Brown"* and Jenny Diver in *"Three Penny Opera."*

Theater was definitely my passion, but was it really what I wanted for my life?

You see, there was a minor hitch. I also had dreams of spending my life with G-Man—hubby now for thirty-seven years. No way would he follow me to the Big Apple, a city as foreign to us two provincials as Budapest. What should I do?

I tried to sort it out. I'd always yearned for Broadway, but I knew dreams were often more attractive than reality. The answer was to rework those dreams: I could continue my music as a hobby and have G-Man too.

G-Man and I have had a great life in our small town. Over the years I've had chances to sing almost everywhere a tune was needed—including those quiet moments as I rocked and nursed our four precious children. Life's been good. No dream could be better.

This fall our community theatre produced *"Nunsense,"* and I played Sister Amnesia, the goofy one. The role was challenging for middle-aged, forgetful me. Frantically poring over lines and lyrics every off-stage moment, I nevertheless found it satisfying to perform for friends and family who loved me whether my tootle was tuned or not.

Afterwards, son Will said, "Mom, I didn't know you could do that."

Well, son, it's like this. There are lots of things about us mamas and our abilities that are not generally known—even to our families.

Mamas are good for more than folding clothes and throwing a roast in the oven. And while your mama is sweeping the front walk and humming a tune, sometimes she's not there at all. Sometimes she's far away. On a stage. And the audience is clapping . . . and clapping.

But Mama hums and smiles and knows she was lucky, immature as she was at the time, to have chosen the path that led her straight to a most satisfying and blessed life.

Good Wife's Horse Tale

Recently, while mounted on a gentle horse named Eli, in the company of hubby G-Man and two others, I journeyed through the silk of new fallen snow in the Smoky Mountains. Granted, I not so much rode the horse as was conveyed, but the fact remains: I did it.

We were at Blackberry Farm in the Smokies for a short winter vacation, and my horseman spouse was determined we were going on a trail ride. His motto is akin to that of Daniel Boone: "All you need for happiness is a good horse and a good wife."

He's definitely got the good wife.

Shivering in 30 degree temperature, this good wife waddled to the stables wrapped in swaddling clothes—long johns, turtleneck, wool sweater, thick socks, jeans, boots and gloves, an extra poofy jacket, and hat with black fur all around my face.

Our guide, a cute cowboy named Jim who once trained elephants (how appropriate, I thought, as I adjusted a couple of my layers) met us at the door. The horses, already saddled, waited in an orderly line, nose to rump, inside the barn.

Truly, I'm one who can differentiate the front end of a horse from the rear, but that's about it. Tough John Wayne once said that "courage is being scared to death and saddling up anyways." Unfortunately, scared to death didn't near 'bout describe my equestrian misgivings.

"Come on in," said Jim. "Get out of the cold."

Good idea, I thought. Maybe we can heat up some cocoa and tell stories. No sense subjecting the horses to this snowy ordeal.

But who's got sense? Especially not Jim and G-Man and the other guy who showed up to ride with us. (He was trying to conquer his fear, he said, since he'd recently been bucked by a steed in San Antonio. He proudly showed me the forty-eight stitches in his right jaw.)

"Ma'am," said Jim, "Eli there is your horse."

Eli turned to look at my black furred head. He snorted.

"Don't mind him," Jim said, "he's looking at your hat. He thinks you're a bear."

I just said "OH." But my mind was racing faster than my conversational skills. How could I abort this folly? I could feign a headache—that usually worked. Or I could claim I was nauseated, which I was truly close to being. Or I could stand my ground and say to G-Man, "Look, sweets. Over there's your good horse. You don't need a good wife at the moment. I'm outta here."

But I didn't. And the snow continued to fall—a heavenly, paradisal vision.

We mounted (OK, OK, I had to use steps) and headed out. We had just lost sight of the barn when we came to a roaring creek. No exaggeration. Icy cold and roaring.

"Follow me," Jim hollered. Shutting my eyes, I grabbed the horn thingy on the saddle. Into the creek we went, into the turbulent waters. Eli slipped and slid on the rocks, but we made it across, and I felt exhilaration only a survivor, or perhaps a conqueror, could feel.

Our ride continued into the mountains, some trails slanting at a precarious 50 degrees or worse. We slogged upward and then down again through muddy clay and slippery leaves. Fallen tree branches, drifts of snow, stones and roots hindered our progress. The horses stumbled but never fell.

"Hey," Jim called to me as Eli paused to nibble tender green fir shoots, "look waaay down there at those rhododendron bushes, wouldja? They'll bloom like crazy long 'bout July."

I peeped. The drop-off was dizzying.

"Man," sighed G-Man, astride his feistier horse, Dancer, "these mountains are something, aren't they?"

I looked at him through my fogged glasses, wiped my nose, and murmured, "Yeah, something." And I meant it.

Two hours later, with aching boo-tay and frozen toes, I slid off Eli in the shelter of the barn. Silently I thanked God for delivering me safe and sound, for helping me make a dent in my paralyzing, cautious nature, and for giving me an opportunity to ride this patient horse, viewing spectacular mountain vistas cloaked in lacy blankets of snow.

It's been said one can get in a car and see what man has made . . . or one can get on a horse and see what God has made.

This good wife can vouch for that.

Granny Goddess

"Nobody can do for little children what grandparents do.
Grandparents sort of sprinkle stardust over the lives of
little children." — Alex Haley

So you think your holidays are topsy-turvy, huh? Having the December crazies? Feeling pooped and draggy? Bemoaning extra pounds already parked in crowded places?

Well, maybe you'll feel better after you read this.

Thanksgiving Day and several days before and beyond, hubby G-Man and I were blessed with the company of our four children, their spouses, and the six grandchildren: Meredith, 7; Wayne, 5; Beth, 3; twin boys, Wilkins and Jacks, 10 months; and Caroline, 7 months.

Count the grandkids.

That's three in the rambunctious-questioning-arguing stage and three in the dirty diapers-spitting up-throwing food stage. A lot for one house.

We turned the place over to them. G-Man parked our RV in the driveway, affording the two of us a perfect sleeping suite and get-away spot.

On the day after Thanksgiving, he left me half snoozing in our cozy cubicle, fought his way into the house, and soon returned to the RV with the morning paper and two cups of coffee.

"I wouldn't advise you to go in there," he said. "It's spelled B-E-D-L-A-M."

That's how things had gone all week, but I must report that smiles were more plentiful than headaches. In spite of the bumps and bangs and near misses with poisonous substances that should have been removed earlier by a more watchful grandmother, there were many memorable moments and funny comments from the grandkids—especially five year old Wayne, who never fails to leave this wordsmith speechless.

I was bath supervisor one night, for example, and was attempting to hurry

Wayne. He was humming and loitering and driving me nuts.

"Bebe," he said, "I can't hurry. I'm soaping my favorite arm."

Well, thank goodness for Wayne and his quirky comments. He certainly soothed my spirits the last day of their visit.

In a weak moment, I took the three older grandchildren shopping. As we were checking out of one store, the clerk said to me, "Has anyone ever told you that you look like Jamie Lee Curtis?"

I'm not really up on Jamie Lee Curtis, but I know she has short, dark hair and a long face, so I could imagine a near-sighted stranger might make such a comparison. I was quite flattered and couldn't wait to tell my daughters when I got home.

Their reaction?

"Hey," one said, "that's cool. Jamie Lee Curtis is not that cute, but she has a great body."

Not cute? Are we talking . . . ugly? Or, perhaps, just pitifully plain?

Well, that burst my bubble since I knew the clerk could not possibly have been referring to a "great body" resemblance. I said not a word about my deflated ego and went on about the business of wiping noses and wee bottoms.

Later that afternoon I was explaining to Wayne that the little necklace he got from one of those cheapie quarter machines at the drug store was probably not one his dad would want him to wear.

"Honey," I explained, "that necklace says 'Goddess'—a goddess is like a pretty lady, and you're a boy."

"Oh, that's OK, Bebe," he said. "Daddy won't care. I'm just gonna wear it to remember you after you die."

Well, now, I ask you: Do I really need to care about sharing a dog-face with Jamie Lee Curtis when my five year old grandson sees the word "goddess" and thinks of me?

Nosirree—a granny goddess is just about as good as it gets.

Verily, like many of you, I'm feeling topsy-turvy, pooped and draggy. Holiday frazzled.

After all, I've been washing towels and sheets, picking up puzzle pieces, and scraping dried banana off my kitchen floor for a solid week.

I've kissed away a bucket of tears and bandaged a hundred nasty boo-boos, told endless stories and sung songs till there's no more tunes in the tootle.

Exhausting work, this goddess stuff.

Grouchy Grammarian

"I never made a mistake in grammar but one
in my life and as soon as I done it I seen it."
— Carl Sandburg

Like, listen, I'm like going to like step on a few toes. I have to do that every now and then to satisfy my savage instincts.

And what's my beef today? Well, the "bottom line" is that overused words and phrases are like "driving me nuts"—words and phrases like "like," for example.

And how about "you know"? Is this not the worst filler in conversations when the speaker is lazy brained?

"I wanted to tell her, you know, that if she didn't start, you know, parking her Dodge Dart in the garage, you know, that I would most likely back into it, you know, again."

Two books by author Robert Fiske address the problem of what he calls "dimwitticisms." He defines these as "worn-out expressions that dull our reason and dim our insight, formulas that we rely on when we are too lazy to express what we think or even to discover how we feel."

These two books are *The Dictionary of Concise Writing: 10,000 Alternatives to Wordy Phrases* and *The Dimwit's Dictionary: 5,000 Overused Words and Phrases and Alternatives to Them.*

I picked up both books while I was visiting in Mobile with my children, and [grumble, grumble] Fiske hits the "proverbial nail on the head" (ouch!), alerting me to dozens of mistakes I've made writing this column over the last few years.

Henceforth you will not read "thingie" in any future column of mine. Or "plethora." Or "24/7."

The first time I heard "24/7," meaning open 24 hours a day, 7 days a week,

I grabbed it. Cool lingo doesn't come my way often. I used it often. So does everybody else. The phrase is banned, folks. Wiped out. Done.

I will also never again write "free gift" or "qualified expert" or "possible choices." Fiske maintains a real gift is always free, a real expert is always qualified, and nobody with sense is going to consider impossible choices.

Following my sons' athletic endeavors over the years I've groaned over these two bits of sports talk: "I told the boys somebody had to step up and do something." And "We just want to go out there and have a good time." C'mon, coaches, pitch these weary words.

Then last week I chanced on an article about travel writing. The author bemoaned the fact that, along with "rustic" and "quaint," writers love to use the adjective "charming." I chuckled aloud as I read one of the examples:

"I don't think I'll ever forget the sound of a 32-foot houseboat slamming against the inside wall of a charming stone bridge."

That would be jarring for the charming stones, I'm sure.

And do the obituary write-ups catch your attention as they do mine? And do you grin inappropriately over repetitive, fill-in-the-blank statements like this? "Mrs. Anderson, 102, was preceded in death by her parents."

I 'spect they got that right.

But don't be worrying yourself over all this. There are folks who fight dimwitticisms in this world of ours. They're doing their best against all odds.

Since 1976 the English faculty at Lake Superior State University has published an annual "Banned Words" list compiled from nominations sent in from all over the world. This year there were over 3,000 nominees for their string of words banished for "Mis-Use, Over-Use, and General Uselessness."

They invite us all to mail in our favorites. Which I've done. And what's that?

Like the drip, drip, drip of the drops in water torture, the repetition of the word "awesome" drives me up the wall. (Drives me up the wall? Sorry, can't say it any better.)

My senior English teacher, Effie Glassco, hated the word "wonderful." She'd say: "The vacation is wonderful. The movie date is wonderful. The wastebasket is wonderful. Pshaw!"

And that's how I feel about "awesome." Use it and reuse it, over and over, and there's no impact left. No oomph. No zip. No real meaning.

Overused words and phrases are no more than thingies. And that's the bottom line from a qualified expert.

Halloween Cynic

There once was a time over three decades ago when I thought a raucous Halloween celebration was the absolute cartwheel of innocent romps.

Hubby G-Man and I were newly married in the fall of 1966. I was young, green, and could not wait for life's little rituals to enfold in my very own home. I'd have a seasonal wreath on the door, a burping coffee percolator, and welcoming activities proclaiming to the world that "herein lives a happy homemaker."

These welcoming activities did indeed develop nicely, including invitations to door-to-door Electrolux salesmen (couldn't afford the vacuum but got free rug cleanings), encyclopedia pushers (couldn't afford those either, but—much to G-Man's distress--bought), and, for a brief time, trick-or-treaters.

Halloween during my numero uno marriage year was to be a big deal in our teensy barracks-like apartment in Avent Acres, Oxford, Mississippi. I dangled a few dime store plastic bats at the front door, carved a jagged toothed jack-o-lantern, and poured a sack of candy corn into a basket.

I thought about greeting the visitors with a sheet over my head—no, not as a ghost; I would be an "unmade bed."

This idea was vetoed quickly when I realized, due to our status as struggling students, I couldn't be poking eye holes in either of our bed sheets.

But there I was on October 31, 1966, about to enjoy Halloween in our wee "early attic" apartment. Darkness descended. I lit the pumpkin candle and readied for the parade of masqueraders.

Then I turned on the porch lights. Our brilliantly lit home was a beacon in the night to hungry trick-or-treaters.

While G-man studied, I waited with much anticipation, enjoying flashbacks to childhood Halloweens when we tricksters scurried around the neighborhood in our princess and cowboy costumes. We were inevitably treated each year at Doodie Wyatt's with hot chocolate and at Louise Warner's with popcorn balls and peanut butter on saltines.

I remembered how Mrs. Peckenpaugh always decorated her garage and let us kids bob for apples, play "Pin the Witch on the Broom," and grab handfuls of Cracker Jacks from a big bucket.

(Isn't it funny how we remember the good things and forget the stomach aches?)

Well, finally my Avent Acres bandits began to arrive.

The first fifteen rings of the doorbell were rather exhilarating. The tots were cute and polite, their costumes creative and amusing.

However, after approximately one hour of jumping up and down to answer the door and listening to G-Man grumble about how in the world (well, it went something like that) he was going to learn Constitutional Law with all this distraction, I was ready to shut the Halloween thing down.

I confess I've never really gotten my trick-or-treating gumption recranked. There are no popcorn balls and hot chocolate at my house, and I may have a plastic pumpkin, but don't count on it.

The truth is (at least, I heard a CNN commentator proclaim) that most adults really dislike Halloween, which I find hard to believe when I see the throngs of customers rifling through racks of costumes at the marts.

If most of us hate this holiday, how come it's such big business?

Halloween is an old Druidic ritual, but how many Druids do you know in our parts? Maybe they're the short ones disguising themselves as Ninja Turtles and Little Mermaids, begging for sweets at our front doors. I don't know.

I do know that Halloween sells. I figure, quite frankly, this is because it's the only time of year people can be deliberately nasty and get away with it.

Want to growl at the world as an alien, a monster, a mummy, a goblin, a revolting ghoul? You can.

The drama. That's what it is—a catharsis of that pent up stress we harbor. And it's all great fun. Unless you come to my house.

So, bah humbug to Halloween. Don't think you can dress up as an Electrolux salesman and get me to open the door.

Our lights are out. Our beacon is broken. Go next door; they've got a bucket of Cracker Jacks.

Head Cheerleader

> "If you don't learn anything but self-discipline,
> then athletics is worthwhile."
>
> — Coach Bear Bryant

Several weeks ago in the grocery store I found myself staring at an adorable child. He was spinning in circles, his rust colored hair atangle, his muscular little arms ending in fists that pummeled the air as he spun down the aisle. And on the back of his shirt was the name of his team, ROWDIES, and his number, 3.

My heart jumped. I swallowed hard and went on about my business selecting just the right shredded wheat for hubby G-Man's breakfast, but it's a wonder I didn't collapse in a heap, all joogled up inside, for once upon a time we had rowdies, and over the years the number 3 was more often than not the beloved number we cheered.

It's like this.

Season after season G-Man and I sat through the trauma/ecstasy of watching our two sons play football and baseball in high school and then baseball at Millsaps College. We spent hours in cheering sections at the ball field even before this though, the boys in park commission ball and the girls in softball and cheerleading. Yep, we were bleacher bums for over twenty-five years, starting with tee ball and moving right along till the tears of that very last "Mom-and-Dad-are-with-you-babe" game with all four children.

I must admit I suffered from withdrawal my first year out of the stands. It wasn't easy. Other avid sports moms will support me on this: When the end comes you hurt probably more than your child.

Usually the kids are ready to move on, but not you. You cling to those golden memories of games children play—the roar of the crowd as the cheerleaders charge on the field, the thrill of the stolen base, the touchdown pass.

You remember how you sat in those bleachers, crossing your fingers till your knuckles were white and cramped, trying to stay calm while your heart pounded with every triumph and practically stopped with every mishap.

I think about this a lot as I pass the football and baseball fields down the street from our house.

I see kids playing their hearts out, and I remember how G-Man and I followed our teams from here to yonder, hooting and hollering and cheering.

Now I envy the parents I see loading their cars and trucks with all the paraphernalia necessary for ultimate bleacher comfort, and find myself wishing I could turn the clock back and cheer my kids one more time—watch Will steal one more base, watch Tom take the mound one more time, watch them both run the option or throw a touchdown pass, watch Emily and Bethany shake those pom poms and lead one more "Two Bits!"

You know, end of the year athletic awards go to the athletes, but parents deserve a mention, don't we?

I mean, who birthed these stalwart young men and agile young ladies?

Who washed those uniforms at 1:00 in the morning?

Who raced to the school toting jerseys accidentally left by the kitchen door?

Who huddled in the rain, drenched to the skin, coughing and sneezing, refusing to move till the last buzzer?

Who suffered burns and ugly fever blisters from the bite of the blazing sun?

Who loved every minute of it and would do it again in a heartbeat?

Guess.

High Heels Get Pitcheroo

"It's those things that seem like
almost nothing that can, in the end,
nearly kill you." — Angela Warner

Those up-east citizens are at it again. This time the news media folks are buzzing about a Connecticut gal they're calling Bridezilla. Seems Bridezilla went berserk at her wedding reception and began throwing Italian cream cake and gifts all over the place. The police had to come and arrest her to stop the rampage. As they hauled her off to jail she tried to sink her teeth into an officer's arm while she kicked the door and window of the police cruiser.

Now, that's rowdy.

But the girl was mad, and I know exactly what happened. The problem, I'm surmising, had to do with her feet.

If you're a woman, you've been there. You've felt the pain. It's those blame high heels. After an hour or two they'll drive even the mildest mannered girl to commit mayhem.

Marilyn Monroe once cooed, "I don't know who invented high heels, but all women owe him a lot."

Yeah, like a turnip up his nose.

My friend Mary has a new job in Memphis. Would you believe one of the requirements is that she wear high heels? No kidding. And this job is with the school system. She's now a supervisor and has to look professional, she says.

I'm wondering how anybody looks professional when they're hobbling from one supervisory location to another.

And do you know that high heels cause your boo-tay to stick out an additional 25%? How professional looking is that?

(Hey, I'm talking about legitimate professions.)

A publication called *Health and Age* maintains that high heels are the "major cause of foot problems in women. Many fashionable high heels are designed to constrict the foot by up to an inch. One study even suggests that wearing heels may lead to arthritis of the knee."

So why do we women do this to ourselves?

Because fashion designers like Stuart Weitzman feed us a bunch of hogwash.

"Nothing has been invented yet," he says, "that will do a better job than high heels at making a good pair of legs look fabulous."

I say what good are a fabulous pair of legs if I can't walk?

I read where Miss Mississippi is having to wear 7 1/2" heels for the Miss America pageant. What? Since when has it become attractive to parade on stilts? This is really putting our Miss on a pedestal, right?

Quite frankly, my little two inch heels are close to being thrown in the trash. I'm tired of all this pain for the sake of what? Looking cute? Duh-ream on.

So what am I going to wear on my feet other than my good ol' sneakers?

I saw a story about a man named Hlavacek who's reconstructed a pair of shoes found on the feet of the prehistoric iceman whose mummified body was discovered in an Alpine glacier. The soles of the shoes are of thin bearskin, padded on the inside with hay. This, I like.

Or maybe I'll fill my closet with the cutest shoe I've seen in a long time— a balloon adorned flip flop.

The college girl who bounced past me in a restaurant stopped to show me the flip flops when I grabbed her arm and exclaimed, "Those sandals are adorrrrrable!"

She created them herself, she said. She bought a pair of inexpensive flip flops at a discount store, then tied colorful balloons (not blown up, of course), bunched closely, on the strap part. Talk about flouncy and pert.

And, may I add, comfortable.

Yep, I've got a plan—a road trip to Albany, Indiana. There on their little town square is a shoe tree. Locals and tourists have tossed hundreds of shoes up in that oak tree for years, and I understand it's something to see.

Maybe Bridezilla would join me in pitching our ouchers up in the Albany shoe tree. Then we could run by the dollar store and invest in some flip flops.

Reckon I can find balloons in fall colors?

Highway Divas

"You may have heard of jalopies,
You heard the noise they make,
My Rocket 88 . . ."

Driving home the other day from one of those whirlwind, overnight visits south to stock up on hugs and kisses from grandchildren, I was juking and jiving and singing along with the radio. I'd found a station of "Oldies" music from the '50s and '60s, and I sounded so doggone good I could hardly stand it. Coolest thing on the road—croaks, cracks, and all.

Gladys Knight and I had just finished singing a rousing duet of *"Midnight Train to Georgia (wooo! wooo!)"* when the disc jockey came on, talking about a song called *"Rocket 88."* Ever heard it?

Seems that "Rocket 88," produced in 1951, has been called the very first rock & roll song. The DJ went on to say that this song was recorded by Ike Turner and his band for Memphian Sam Phillips, who later sold the record to the larger Chess label.

Why did this information blow my skirt?

Because my dear friend and right arm around our Jacks household, Daisy Gibson Brandon, along with her Clarksdale, Mississippi, beau, Johnny, used to double date with Ike Turner and his girlfriends during the early '50s.

"He was a nice man back then," Daisy told me the next day when I quizzed her, urging her to remember fifty year old events to give me some story material.

"One Sunday night his band was playing in Inverness. Johnny and I went with him, because wherever Ike played there was a good time. I remember that night in particular because he kept teasing me, saying 'Daisy, you gonna sing with the Kings of Rhythm tonight!' Now, I could dance and sing, but I was only 16 years old and real shy. I was scared to death he was gonna make me get up there and sing."

Izear Luster (Ike) Turner, Jr., was born in Clarksdale in 1931. It's amazing to me that this man is over 70 years old today and still performing, enjoying recognition from the Grammy and W. C. Handy Awards. He and his one-time partner, Tina Turner, have also been inducted into the Rock & Roll Hall of Fame.

Hubby G-Man and I happened to be staying at a New Orleans hotel one weekend in the '80s when Tina Turner launched her solo comeback. She was performing at the hotel lounge, and, deciding we'd rather see Tina than Bourbon Street, we soon found ourselves seated within arm's length of the stage.

Friends, if there's another way to spell E-N-E-R-G-Y, it's T-I-N-A. She was spectacular. This woman, at least 40 years old at the time, never quit. She twirled, she pranced, she kicked, she shimmied—and all the time she was belting songs ninety to nothing. She sounded fabulous and looked even better.

"So, Daisy," I said, "did you double date with Tina?"

"No," she said, "that must have been later."

I looked it up, and Daisy was right.

Ike met Tina in St. Louis in the late '50s. She was Annie Mae Bullock then, a quiet teenager from around Brownsville, Tennessee, who just stepped to the stage one night and sang with Ike's band. Ike changed her name to Tina Turner, and the rest of the story is chronicled by Tina in her book *I, Tina* and the resulting movie, *What's Love Got To Do With It?* (1993). Ike has also written his own book, *Takin' Back My Name* (1998), in which he disputes much of Tina's account of their troubles.

"Just think, Daisy," I said. "If you'd sung with Ike's band that night in Inverness, today YOU might be Tina Turner!"

She turned and grinned. I thought she was getting ready to protest my outrageous hypothesis, but she didn't bat an eye as she nodded and said, "Yeah, you probably right."

I have an idea Daisy found herself a good "Oldies" station as she drove up Highway 61 on the way home that evening. I figure she was most probably singing her heart out with Dionne or Lavern or somebody.

That's what we Divas do.

Holiday Memories

"Over the river and through the woods, to Grandmother's house we go..."

Do grandmothers still knock themselves out to feed the whole hoot-and-hollerin' family on Thanksgiving Day?

Some do.

My friend Frankie is feeding fifty-four folks on Turkey Day. Whew. The very thought makes me want to curl into fetal position under a stack of "blankies" and hide from the world. Is she nuts? Or is she making holiday memories?

There's got to be a better way to create memories. Fifty-four family members and assorted friends counting on my congealed salad to congeal?

I don't think so.

Besides, my own childhood memories of Thanksgivings-past center not just on the food of the day but on the camaraderie of sing-a-longs, pecan gathering (beaning annoying cousins), football games, and Scrabble contests anchored by endless conversation among the aunts and uncles.

My holiday memories even include a few shenanigans. Here's one.

My beloved grandfather, James Hardy Holder of Iuka, Mississippi, a retired Methodist minister, was forever bringing home itinerant preachers for dinner on holidays as well as plain ole everyday days.

Unlike her cooking-impaired granddaughter (me) who goes into spasms of topsyturvydom at the thought, Granny never seemed to blink an eye at these "no notice" invitations.

One Thanksgiving back in the 50's, here came Granddaddy, shuffling onto the back gallery and pushing through the kitchen door with two fellows—both Methodist preachers, bachelors most likely, en route from one camp meeting or revival to another, stopping as usual at Brother Holder's. Didn't make a bit of difference to them or to Granny that this was Thanksgiving Day. Another soul just meant that much more merriment.

Granny and Granddaddy had a big dining table with room enough for our whole family—until the visiting ministers showed up. Their arrival meant there were two less places to sit for a couple of us kids.

And so it was that my sister Kathy and I were placed at a small table near the stairway. We sat alone and finished our meal while the folks at the big table were still going at it, enjoying their holiday feast in fine and extended style.

Kathy and I decided we'd slip up the stairs and discover something more interesting to do. And we did.

Hanging from the stairway's second floor ceiling was a really long string with a metal tip. When pulled, the string turned on a naked lightbulb, which, of course, was not lit during this beautiful holiday dinner.

Perched on the darkened stairs and with just the right flick of our wrists, we could swing the string through the bannisters in the direction of the bald head of one of the visitors. We took turns.

Tat. Tat. Tat. Tat.

We pecked the interloping Reverend on his shiny head over and over with that metal tip. He swatted at this mysterious annoyance, wondering, I'm sure, what kind of pesky insects were invading Brother Holder's parsonage when the frost had obviously already settled on the pumpkin.

Granny was ever vigilant, however. Noticing the discomfort of her guest, she soon rose from her seat, quietly made her way up the stairs, and brought down two remorseful (but giggling) little girls.

Yes indeed, I don't remember what we ate at the festive meal that day, but I'm guessing we had delicious servings of turkey and dressing, asparagus casserole, bing cherry salad, and Granny's famous pecan pie. I don't remember, because the food, you see, was important, but not MOST important.

More significant were the laughter and hugs that welcomed two little pranksters as we joined the jovial group at the dining table that Thanksgiving Day fifty long years ago. More important was the fun we all had together.

This is my justification for not spending every waking moment in the kitchen during the holidays, I suppose, but I DO plan to serve up lots of chuckles and hugs.

Years from now somebody will be glad I did.

Somebody might be remembering.

Honey, You're Not Going To Believe This!

Many years ago my hubby G-Man and I had a long discussion on a most important subject regarding a form of immersing oneself in hot water.

Most of us deal with this "getting into hot water" every day of our lives. Sometimes we endure great embarrassment because of it. Usually we experience terrible confusion. Often insomnia results.

This horrible condition called I-Know-The-Face-But-I-Can't-Remember-The-Name has happened to all of us.

It's no fun.

G-Man and I were discussing the best way to handle such a situation.

Honest gal that I am, I said the best way to handle it is to say right up front, "Oh, my goodness. I know your face but I can't remember your name." Then hug bigtime, maybe even plant a sloppy smooch on the person's cheek when the name is spoken, and squeal: "Of course, [I think] I remember you!"

G-Man said no way. The man is a semi-politician, see. He knows almost everybody around, and he said there was no way he would embarrass folks by telling them he couldn't remember something as important to them as their very names.

He said all one has to do is shake hands and mumble a little so the person *thinks* you've said his name.

We argued back and forth, but he's a lawyer/mouthpiece and I can't ever win, so I hushed.

A few days after that heated discussion we went to Silver Dollar City in Missouri with our four children for a short vacation. After lugging umpteen bags into our cozy cabin we headed for . . . where else? The goofy golf course.

G-Man took the kids down to play goofy golf while I stayed with a book in a shady area with benches.

You should know that I can get the data of a stranger's life history before a stick of Juicy Fruit goes stale, so within ten minutes I was chatting away with my benchmate.

This nice lady, a Kansan, was visiting Silver Dollar Divine Destination and Tourist Haven with her family. She was waiting for her goofy golfing kids while her husband attended a dental seminar.

We hit it off right away.

"Hey," I said, "would you help me play a trick on my husband?"

"Sure," she said.

I put the game plan before her and she was all for it. So this woman I'd never laid eyes on in my life proceeded to hike down to the goofy golfers with me.

"Gerald!" I hollered. "Hold up a minute. You're not going to believe this. Look who's here!"

I pointed to the lady. G-Man looked blank.

"Is this not something?" I said. "She just walked up out of the blue. What a coincidence!"

While G-Man's brow began to furrow, I grabbed and hugged the living daylights out of my lady-partner-in-crime.

The children stood there with their little golf clubs. I heard one whisper to her siblings: "Oh, boy, Mama's found another cousin."

I could see wheels turning in G-Man's head.

After several seconds his face brightened. He patted the lady's arm and gushed, "Well, brurmphstf. How are you? It's been a long time."

"Sure has," she said.

"Uh," he stammered, "how have you been?"

"Fine," she said. (Gosh, she was magnificent.)

"You here at Silver Dollar City on vacation?"

"Yes, Ron and the children and I are here for a dental seminar."

Dental. Dental. Dental. Ron. Ron. Ron who? Who can this be?

I could see the words somersaulting in his brain.

Well, the torture was too great. I couldn't stand to see the man suffer, so I started laughing like crazy. The lady did too, and he knew he'd been had.

G-Man's face flushed like a barrel of ketchup. He tried to be a good sport, but he was stewing; however, I've maintained to this day he got exactly what he deserved at that goofy golf course. Yes, indeed.

Hey, Brurmphstf, are you out there, girl? Are you still grinning?

I'm A What?

I had a wonderful childhood growing up in my little Mississippi town—a hardworking, loving C.P.A. dad; a creative, fun-loving, stay-at-home mom; an older brother I worshiped; two younger sisters who did everything I told them to do and loved me anyway.

There are few things I remember as real disappointments during those formative years; however, one crushing experience I still recall was the time I was a mushroom.

You got it. A mushroom.

The year was 1954, I was in fourth grade at Delta State's Hill Demonstration School, and time came for the spring pageant. All my little girlfriends were flowers or butterflies or birdies; they wore scarlet and lilac and baby blue. I wore an ugly brown polished cotton costume with ridiculous pink ruffles underneath—the kind of thing you'd expect a mushroom to wear to twirl in circles.

Mama said I looked just fine, but I knew better.

Judy was a bluebird—she had tiny blue feathers entwined in her braids. Ann and Delia were flowers—they had blossoms sprinkled in their curls.

But me? There were no hair options for a mushroom. I didn't look pretty and I knew it.

To make matters worse, there were only two other girl mushrooms, and the rest of this motley crew of fungi were [gasp] boys—including my friend Jim, who graciously helped me recall the sordid details of this ordeal.

I was a smart kid though; I knew there was not a tittle of a chance to argue successfully with steely Ethel Cain, the phys ed director, so there I was, taking my place on the school lawn as the grimmest mushroom in the bunch.

Ann and Delia were always a little spacey, so they didn't realize how disappointed I was.

Judy, though, was a different story. She was the first of us to get toe shoes and dance on her toes, and she was always the featured one—the Little Miss Muffet, the Cinderella, the Sleeping Beauty.

Well, as I found my spot beside the hedge on the left with the others of our drab group, Judy fluttered by.

"Hi, toadstools!" she whispered.

Huh? Low blow, for sure.

I'd like to say this story has a happy ending, but it doesn't. For one miserable evening I was an embarrassed, self-conscious, unattractive toadstool.

I suppose the experience helped toughen me for future disappointments.

There have been many times I've felt like a toadstool/mushroom over the years, but I've learned those down times do end. The music stops, the lights go off, and I can go home to cuddle in my bed and wake to a new day.

Nobody has to twirl in humiliating circles forever.

There. That's my mushroom advice for today. No charge.

Jewelry Laws Rescue Country Girl

Julia Reed hails from Greenville, Mississippi. She's been in New York City for a number of years now, writing for magazines and newspapers—a southern girl in remote mode, so to speak—and she knows some stuff. So I paused when I read where she's quoted as saying: "The deep-dyed fear that lives in the heart of every Southerner, myself included, [is] that a Yankee is putting us down."

Naaa, not so, I think. But then I remember my shameful experience several weeks ago and realize Julia's not far off the mark.

Should I tell what I did? Oh, why not.

OK, here's the deal. I was in New York with hubby G-Man. He left to go off into the bowels of the city to meet with a bunch of lawyers (what fun!) and I planned to while away the day, mostly resting and reading.

I was enjoying Bobbie Ann Mason's CLEAR SPRINGS, and got to the part where she graduates from the University of Kentucky and heads to New York.

"I craved change and excitement," she wrote. "Going to the big city did not seem bold or brave to me. It merely seemed inevitable . . . But this was New York, where people from the rural South could be dismissed as hicks . . . gullible."

Hicks? Gullible? Me? Never.

After a while I slapped myself upside the head and thought, girl, you can read at home—get your provincial self out on the avenue with these N'Yorkers. So I headed out in my Easy Spirits for a good walk north on Madison. I strolled sixteen blocks up to 68th Street, window shopping along the way, then crossed the street and started south.

What's hard about this? I thought. I can walk as briskly as any of these folks. I'm southern, but I'm no slouch. I can even go with the flow and cross the street when I'm not supposed to. Who's hickish? Not me.

So, see, block by block, I was overcoming my country girl inferiority complex.

By the time I got sixteen blocks back down Madison to 52nd Street, I was thinking I was pretty slick. I noticed a shop with a fancy Italian name and went in. I was the only customer. At least, the three salesladies thought I was a customer, so they began to hover.

"These are designer copies of fine jewelry," one said. "Every piece is made in Italy."

"Yes," cooed another, "you know it's not wise to travel with your jewels."

The third, her brows and lips penciled so distinctly I began to wonder if she was a mannequin, stood watch over the cash drawer.

For some unexplained reason, their hoity-toitiness triggered a bit of mischief in my prankster brain.

"Look," said the first lady, holding out an arm cum bracelet. "We have these exquisite bracelets made of teakwood and set with hyacinth stones. No one would ever know they're not really diamonds."

The devil made me do it.

I looked at her bracelet, sighed, and said, "Oh, I'm afraid we have these little idiosyncrasies in the South that would prevent my purchasing a bracelet like that."

The mannequin perked up. The other two moved closer.

"You do?" they said.

"Oh, yes," I continued. "The teakwood has an informal look, which would be nice for day wear. But then you've added the mock jewels, and I'm sure you were taught, as was I, that you wear glittering jewels only to formal events in the evening, never in the daytime."

"You don't?" they said, their painted lips frozen in teensy O's.

I gave these dear ladies a big smile and headed out the door of their fake shop with my fake southern sophistication.

What they didn't realize was that they actually could have stuck emerald studs in the ends of their pointed noses at high noon and I would have said, "Go on, sister. Do your thing."

Was I fearful, as Julia Reed expressed, that I might step into a fancy-dancy Yankee shop and they would "put me down" because of my southern ways?

Yeah, I guess I was, but these women actually were sweet as could be.

And bless their gullible hearts, it's not their fault they don't know the southern jewelry laws.

Junkin' Treasures

Reality television with all its dirt and humiliation is struggling for titillating, slap-your-head thrills. The themes just keep getting wilder and wilder until viewers want to scream, "Junk 'em, puh-lease!"

Have you read about the new reality television show being proposed by CBS? The show, right now in its formative stages, is being called *"The Real Beverly Hillbillies."*

CBS is looking for the perfect Dixieland family—you know, the dummy, snaggle toothed, barefooted Southern stereotype. Producers will set this family up in a swank Beverly Hills mansion, allowing all the world to watch and "enjoy" the shenanigans.

How low can they go? This is definitely one they should junk. I'll watch *"The Real Beverly Hillbillies"* about as much as I watch the other reality shows—which is never.

But hey, speaking of junk, there's another candidate for reality programming that might capture my attention.

This one, set to debut in July, is called *"Junkin."* (Turner South)

Designed to offer breathtaking adventures, *"Junkin"* features a Southern guy with his hip hop female companion as they shop all around the country in junk shops, flea markets and yard sales.

Now, THAT is exciting.

I know about junk shop excitement because several years ago I had one of the craziest experiences of my life in Mr. Fox's Junk Emporium.

My house guest and I were trying to decide how to kill several hours before she had to head to the Memphis airport.

"Why don't we go junkin'?" I said to my guest, Maud van der Sluis, who is from The Netherlands and who knew nothing about the Southern passion for snooping around old collectibles.

She was game, so we headed out.

After browsing through two or three junk shops, I suggested we end our excursion with a visit to Mr. Fox's Junk Emporium, a tiny hole in the wall I'd only visited once years before this day.

I didn't figure the little shop would be of much interest, but we still had an hour to kill.

Sure enough, we circled Mr. Fox's hodgepodge of old junk in fifteen minutes. But then Maud paused beside a box of tattered picture albums and loose clippings. I waited by the door, anxious to leave.

"Look at these photographs," Maud said. "Some are in beautiful leather cases."

"Yeah," I said. "Depressing, isn't it? Those are some family's valuable memories, and now they're shoved back here in this junk shop, selling for little or nothing. Forgotten. Dusty and ruining. That's really sad."

I wanted to add, "Let's go!" But Maud kept studying the pictures.

I leaned against the door, bored to death and antsy.

Finally, I decided if I walked across the room to Maud I could gently steer her away from the cardboard box and out the door.

As she peered at one of the albums, a picture fluttered to the floor. She leaned down to pick it up just as I reached her side. I looked.

There in Maud's hand was a picture of my dad, about fifteen years old, his black curly hair framing a handsome face. He lay on the grass, his chin in his hands.

Grabbing the album, I leafed through the pages

There were more pictures of Dad as a teenager. Pictures of the family home on the hill in Iuka. My Aunt Elizabeth, young and vivacious. My precious grandparents, Jim and Beulah Holder, dressed for church, working in their garden, feeding the chickens.

The cardboard box contained stacks of family photos and clippings. I bought the whole stash of valuable family memories for twenty-five measly bucks.

Apparently this box of memorabilia had been thrown away mistakenly when my mother moved after Dad's death, but here it was months later in this teeny, out-of-the-way shop, waiting for me to come to the rescue.

Maud had never met my parents. Didn't know what they looked like. Her fascination with the pictures was eerie and unexplained.

And never in a million years would I normally have gone to Mr. Fox's Junk Emporium that day. The whole junkin' morning had simply been a spur of the moment decision. A whim.

Or was it?

Turner South can only hope their reality TV shopping couple finds, by luck or perhaps by some more mysterious force, such treasures.

Maalox and Nose Drops and Mean Ol' Handmirrors

Oh, woe. Here comes January, and in a couple of weeks I'll be a year older. Capricorn, that's me. The old goat.

Hubby G-Man passed my bathroom door the other day while I was brushing on a bit of blush/rouge stuff, and he said, "What you doing, honey? Painting a masterpiece?"

I never let up with the project at hand and said, "Nope, just restoring a relic."

Got to keep a sense of humor about this aging business.

My friend Carolyn forwarded to me an "aging" poem which began: "Maalox and nose drops and needles for knitting/Walkers and handrails and new dental fittings/Bundles of magazines tied up in strings/These are a few of my favorite things . . ."

The poem had me hooting, but hey, the final verse emphasized that reaching the "mature years" is actually not so awful. In spite of what some folks think, life does not end with the sighting of a few gray hairs.

Frankly, I think that's just about where life should start.

By the time we turn fifty we get much more comfortable in our skin (if we keep a sense of humor and continue, by hook or crook, our relic restoration).

But it's inevitable when that fiftieth birthday rolls around, then the sixtieth and upward, there's bound to be some rumbling and grumbling from those who think they're on the downhill slide.

The way I figure it, we should turn that sadness to gladness and be tickled we can still kick a few walls.

When I was a girl over fifty years ago, my pals and I could not wait for the day when we'd grow up. We yearned for the freedom aging would bring into our sheltered lives. We giggled as we shared our dreams of becoming big grown-ups, able to do whatever we wanted to do when we wanted to do it.

We'd have men who loved us and babies who needed us and neighbors who sought our advice and company. We'd wear high heels and silk scarves and scarlet nail polish. We couldn't wait for lipstick, powder, and paint.

("Is you is, or is you ain't?")

All of the above clearly identifies me as being of that generation where females' options (we mistakenly thought) centered on securing a good husband and a bungalow with a two car garage. We were chomping at the bit for our Betty Crocker kitchens and smocked daffodil aprons.

Not only did my girlfriends and I yearn impatiently for adulthood and more independence, we also created a special crystal ball into which we could gaze to see ourselves as we would look when the veil of maturity descended.

Sprawling on the bed on our tummies, we hung our heads over the edge and stared at our faces in a handmirror. Somebody told us the images in the mirror would be THE WAY WE'D LOOK when we grew older.

Sure enough, with heads hanging off the bed, we stared into the handmirror and saw flesh falling forward, tiny wrinkles appearing around our mouths, eyes bulging—these were our future faces . . . and the visions weren't that appealing.

So, my advice to maturing women with upcoming birthdays is this: Don't be hanging off any beds clutching handmirrors. Instead, stand proudly with shoulders back, run your fingers through your hair, dab a little "Coral Calypso" on your lips, pinch your cheeks, and go out into the world knowing you're mighty, mighty fine.

Remember, our aging bodies hear everything our minds think . . . and she who laughs lasts.

Mama In Paris

Several years ago my eighty-year-old mother and I decided to take one of those nine day, whirlwind European trips that whisks you through Paris, Florence, and Rome—you know, "Quick, eyes right, there's Notre Dame."

I should have known better than to drag my dear, sweet, stone-deaf mama on an exhausting excursion like that, but she was all for it. We didn't nickname her the "Wild Goose" for nothing.

Well, off we flew into the blue yonder, but by the time the plane swooped over the ocean and alighted in Paris, we were mega pooped. On a nine day trip though, there's no time to dawdle. We were told to take our bags to our rooms, then hustle downstairs to board a bus to see the sights.

I was concerned about Mama, she's no young chick, but she insisted she would do just fine.

So, with our comfy tennies on our feet, we did as we were told, climbed on the bus, and away we went.

First day went fine. Mostly we rode on the bus and looked at stuff out the window. This was A-OK, as we also grabbed little catnaps now and then when the tour guide wasn't disturbing us with commentary.

The next morning though, after a good night's sleep, we were raring to go. Paris, here we come!

Our first stop was the Louvre. We were to spend several hours there, and then we were on our own until sometime after lunch. Following the guide and holding hands, Mama and I headed for the museum, watching curbs for potential tripper spots, enjoying the scenery when we dared glance up.

After purchasing admission tickets there at the Louvre entrance, the group split. We could wander wherever we wanted, but we were to gather by the pyramid outside around lunchtime. Great.

Mama and I took off. There was no sense joining a group with a museum guide; Mama literally can't hear thunder. We tried the little ear phones and they bothered her, so we did a lot of strolling and reading. After an hour or so, I noticed she was doing more sitting than perusing.

"I don't mean to be low brow," Mama said, "but I've seen enough."

Ever tried to do the Louvre in ninety minutes? Well, I admit I was weary too, so we went outside to wait for the rest of the folks in our group.

Eventually they all came out, and we discussed where we'd go for lunch. Several wanted to go one direction, several wanted to go another, and the third group, which I decided to join, wanted to go to Montmartre.

"MAMA," I said to my deaf mother in a voice loud enough to raise Monsieur Napoleon from his tomb, "MAMA, DO YOU WANT TO GO TO MONTMARTRE?"

"Oh, sure. That sounds wonderful," she said.

Off we went to catch the Metro. We reached Montmartre, went up in the little cable car, toured the beautiful Basilique du Sacre-Coeur, then hiked over to the square to check out the artists and shop a bit.

Next to famished by then, we decided to have coffee and a sandwich at an outdoor cafe. Breezes, flowers, music, ancient cobblestones, fascinating architecture—what a splendid day in historic Montmartre. The ambiance of this beautiful spot had seized my very soul. "Ahhh, j'adore! Montmartre, Montmartre—you've captured my poor heart . . ."

While we were munching our croissants, Mama stopped eating, took a sip of her coffee, and patted her mouth with her napkin.

"Honey," she said, "this is really nice, but you remember what you asked me back there at the museum? I mean, I don't want to rush you, but aren't we going to look for a WalMart?"

Y-Y-Y-Yeah.

Mothers and Sons

Is that a gentle breeze wafting through this room, or could it be my own wistful sigh?

The latter, yes. I've just returned to my writing after watching (for the hundredth time) son Tom's wedding video. Tom, the youngest of our four children, married in Colorado, and the video of this beautiful summertime wedding is a real keepsake.

As I sit here, John Denver's "Annie's Song" is still tip-toeing through my brain and wrecked emotions, and when I shut my eyes I still envision the Rockies—a dizzying experience always for this flatlander girl.

I've "done" the Rocky Mountains now for twenty years, and I never make the drive through or flight over without being awestruck anew. I've never quite figured why God gave them such grandeur and gave us clay hills and dirt levees. Something's not quite fair about that.

And the heat. May I gripe?

Here in the Deep South our temperature hovers around 100 degrees in July and August—only bearable because we love this place.

Yes, I do love the Southland dearly, but I think I could get used to the gentle touch of the Rocky Mountains' balmy winds and easy sunshine—especially during the summer.

Nobody will disagree that our temperature here in the Magnolia State has been absolutely awful lately. I tried to work in my day lilies today and almost died, perspiring as no lady properly should.

All right, I thought, I'll use my mind and my senses to transcend/transfer/move beyond this Mississippi humidity. The scent of jasmine and honeysuckle was faint in the air. My knees felt cool as they pressed against the smooth pebbles of the garden path.

I closed my eyes and began to hum *"Annie's Song."*

"You fill up my senses/Like a night in the forest/Like the mountains in springtime/ Like a walk in the rain/Like a storm in the desert/ Like a sleepy blue ocean/You fill up my senses/Come fill me again . . ."

I began to think back to Tom's wedding.

I pictured his laughing face as we rafted on the Colorado River and hiked and ate and sang and danced. I thought of his standing with his arms around his wonderful Katie, so full of love he was about to burst. I thought of the precious little home they share—too far now from Mom and Dad.

And I remember thinking, "Gosh, I used to be his best girl."

"You fill up my senses . . ."

It's just so blasted hot. My eyes are absolutely swimming. What? Tears? No, no, I tell you, it's perspiration, that's all.

Excuse me a sec, okay?

Mothers Say The Darnedest Things

I had two of my grandkids in the backseat of the car as I scooted around town the other day. Wayne, who's a mature five years old, was holding forth, chattering ninety to nothing. His little sister Beth (age four) finally had all she could take.

"Waaayne," she said, "you gotta quit talking 'cause my brain's messing up!"

"Beth," Wayne said, "your brain only messes up when you watch too much TV."

Beth started to protest, but Wayne interrupted.

"Listen to me," Wayne said. "I know 'cause Mama said so."

That exchange set me to thinking about all the things mothers through the generations have proclaimed that, by golly, are the truth, the whole truth, and nothing but the unadulterated truth.

Take my mother, for example.

She was big on good behavior. She'd frown at us and say, "Where there's smoke, there's fire." In other words, if the teacher called from school to report misbehavior, we kids didn't even think about making excuses.

The slightest hint we'd done something wrong meant we might as well pull the switch off the privet hedge as we came in the kitchen door.

She believed in self-confidence—"Can't never could."

How many thousands of times did my siblings and I hear this one! How you gonna know if you can accomplish something if you don't give it a shot? She always encouraged us to go for the gusto—"go whole hog," she'd say.

She warned against bragging and self promotion—"Don't let your mouth get you in trouble. If you're good, folks are going to know it. You don't have to tell 'em." Wise words, those.

The chicken that lays the egg cackles first," she'd say, and we'd know we better quit tattling or the major blame for the transgression would fall on our own shoulders.

But if we kept fussing and fighting, she'd holler, "Y'all quit right now. Your hard heads gonna make soft behinds!"

And, oh, how she did believe in that old goody, "Spare the rod and spoil the child."

She insisted on cleanliness—"Never leave dishes in the sink at night or a bed unmade in the morning." She was a firm believer that cleanliness is next to godliness, and we heard about it. Often.

She instilled in us the belief that "people are just generally good."

Look and you'll find something to like in almost everybody. Oh, she could indulge in spicy gossip like the rest of us, but she was always as good-natured as the day is long.

Whenever we set out on trips without her, she'd call out, "Be careful. Remember you're carrying precious cargo!" How dear is that?

She hugged us and encouraged us and disciplined with love. For every bit of constructive criticism, there was an extra helping of praise.

"Don't settle for mediocrity—you know you can do better!"

She was adamant that her children realize there were "no excuses for missing Sunday School and Church." We were there, rain or shine. Even on vacations we'd show up at the doors of strange (to us) Methodist churches so we could maintain the discipline of our perfect attendance.

"What goes around, comes around." Ahhh, she liked this one. If we girls threw a bucket of hot water out the front door at the Hawkins boys, we could certainly expect to be chased all the way to Yale Street. She didn't feel a bit sorry for us.

All these wise words, often countrified and humorous, were employed to lead us kids down the straight and narrow.

Mama said so. There was no dispute.

Oh, there were a zillion memorable "Mama Instructions"—too many for this short article. But there's one more I definitely can't omit.

Mama always had some special words she still says to this very day every time I leave her retirement home.

"Honey," she says, "remember whose daughter you are."

I always look back at her beautiful, eighty-five year old face and dutifully reply, "Yes, ma'am."

As if I could ever forget such wisdom.

My Cousin, My Friend

It's a Friday afternoon and I'm sitting on the floor of my mother's room at Indywood Personal Care Home. We've recently moved Mama here, and, as she states over and over, she's "happy as a dead pig in the sunshine."

But this day she has aches just annoying enough to keep her on the couch where she's bolstered by pillows and cozied with a light afghan. I sit with her, chatting and arranging family pictures in a new photo album.

Soon we hear a tap on the door. Mama's first-cousin, Bill, has come for a visit. Mama and Bill are a month apart in age, grew up together in Pace, Mississippi, and have been not only cousins but friends for almost eighty-five years.

Bill sits on the ottoman beside Mama and pats her hand.

"Beth," Mama says, her blue eyes twinkling, "Bill's the best cousin. He would just do anything in this world for me."

Bill smiles and laughs and says they surely have had some good times over these many years.

They talk, and Mama's puny feelings almost disappear. Her face glows.

Mama and Bill continue their visit as I sort through pictures. I find a small photo made two summers ago of two of my grandchildren. Meredith (then five) and Wayne (then three), devoted cousins, hold hands as they pose for the camera on a mountain trail in Colorado.

I'm reminded of a conversation between those two that summer as they played in the Colorado wildflowers outside my open kitchen window. Went like this:

"C'mon, Wayne, hold my hand," Meredith said, "I'm gonna show you where the foxes are."

"Uh huh," answered Wayne, the obedient cousin on this particular occasion. Meredith rattles on.

"You 'member the secret passage? That's where we're going. We'll sneak up on the foxes and see the mama shake a mouse to death before she eats it while the daddy fox watches on the big rock . . ."

"Uh huh."

" . . . behind the house."

"Uh huh."

"Mama says she and your mama used to have a secret passage. They played there all the time and nobody, I mean nobody, could find them. That's what we'll do. We'll hide and nobody can find us and we'll live with the foxes down in their deep, deep hole--down there with all their furry babies and we'll eat mice and stuff like that."

[silence]

"Wayne, why aren't you talking?"

[silence]

"Wayne, you don't talk much. Well, doesn't matter 'cause we got to be quiet anyway or we'll scare the foxes and then they'll run off and we . . . You know what, Wayne? I saw the daddy fox and he had scruffy fur and looked terrible, and he probably has some terrible disease and if he bites you then you better watch out and get away from him and really watch out, I mean RE-ALLY watch out, and don't dare get near him and—"

"I'm not going."

"Why, silly? You don't want to see the foxes? They're real cute. They got these long fluffy tails and I promise it's not that gross when the mama fox shakes the mouse and eats it. It doesn't bother me a bit, well, probably 'cause when I saw her she was shaking my cheese toast I threw out the window, not a real mouse, but—"

[wails]

"Oh, okay, forget it. But Wayne, know what? You may be my cousin, but sometimes you just really, really, really 'zasperate me."

I sit there on the floor looking at the picture of Meredith and Wayne, then glance over at Mama and Bill.

My crazy imagination begins to spin, taking me to Pace on a late summer day in 1923. I envision five-year old Edith, my mother, barefooted, in a simple little cotton frock, her blond curls in ringlets framing a scrubbed face.

In my mind I see the child Edith as she grabs the hand of cousin Bill, also five years old, her favorite playmate, a typical little southern boy in his cut-off, grass-stained britches. She pulls him through the rocks and weeds along the bogue bank.

"Hold my hand, Bill" she whispers. "Shhhhh, we got to be quiet. C'mon, I'm gonna show you where the foxes are."

My Rendezvous with Gene Hackman

One ordinary morning several years ago, I was sweeping my kitchen floor when the phone rang. I figured the caller interrupting my domestic chores was probably a pestering telemarketer, but instead I heard the voice of my friend Cathy asking if I wanted to do something interesting the next week—like, be a movie star.

Well, "movie star" has always had a ring to it. Visions of little Breck Shampoo pictures I once carefully cut from magazines back in my childhood danced in my head. Elizabeth Taylor, Barbara Stanwyck, Ann Miller, June Allyson. Glamorous women. I could manage such a thing.

"Sure," I said. I was prepared to answer quickly because I knew the Castlerock movie folks were coming to town to shoot John Grisham's *"The Chamber."* And I knew, actress wannabe that I am, only a brief time would pass before the casting people begged me to join Gene Hackman, Faye Dunnaway and Chris O'Donnell in this film.

Turned out Cathy was joshing. She was phoning from the school superintendent's office, where the movie "getters" had called looking for a tutor for the children on the set. Would I possibly settle, she asked, for "Tutor-On-The-Set" rather than "Movie Star"?

Reluctantly, I agreed, knowing that sometimes one has to get a foot in the door in order, eventually, to tippy-toe into the spotlight.

So, Cathy proceeded with instructions. I was to report to a location out from Itta Bena, Mississippi, at 7 a.m. on Tuesday morning. Itta Bena? Yep, she told me. That was where the location headquarters—the meal tents, the dressing rooms, the administrative trailers—would be. We'd meet there and then pile into buses to drive to the shoot waaaay out in the boonies.

Out in the boonies from Itta Bena? This was going to be interesting, all right.

There was no sleeping the night before. This was my chance. My big break.

❖ 80 ❖

Cinema Cinderella was heading for the ball . . . sorta.

Next morning I was raring to go. I left the house around 6 and headed for Itta Bena. Arriving in this tiny Delta town, I had no trouble finding the location. There were more tents and trailers sitting in the cotton gin parking lot than Itta Beans had ever seen in their lives, I wager. More than I'd ever seen, for sure—but you know how Hollywood overdoes everything.

We got on the yellow school bus and rode for miles. And miles. And have I mentioned the temperature was hovering around 30 degrees? It was. There was no heat on that icebox of a bus, and I was shaking anyway from nerves and excitement. Gene Hackman was waiting for me.

We finally reached the house where filming was to take place. Scheduled to be shot was the opening scene of the movie where Hackman storms out the front door with a shotgun and blasts a guy. Pretty standard fare as movies go. But this meant Hackman spent a lot of time inside the house. With me. And with fifty other people—the skinny wardrobe mistress, the German hairdresser, a dozen runny-nosed children and their mothers, several adult extras, and a bunch of production assistants pulling cords around.

As the Tutor-On-The-Set, I was to baby-sit the children inside the house.

Wrapped in blankets, we all huddled in front of the one space heater. I had been smart enough to wear hubby G-Man's wool hunting cap, a pair of insulated gloves, and several layers of sweaters and jackets. Topped with a couple of blankets, I looked mysteriously chic, so I wasn't surprised when, peeping from my woolen folds, I spied Gene Hackman looking at me from across the room.

He never approached me. Too shy, I guess. But at the time I harbored the fantasy that this great actor relished reshooting the scene over and over so he could get back into that house where I was holding court in front of the space heater.

I realize now he was probably studying my hunkered-up self, trying to decide if that shivering knot of wool hogging the heater was human . . . or a pile of fuzzy blankets with a long nose.

But I never found out for sure. After a gazillion takes, Hackman shot the guy and left, so I left too. I was freezing slap to death and wasn't that set on being a movie star anyway. I resigned my tutor position the next day.

I'm back sweeping the kitchen floor, and, oh shucks, I reckon Hackman's over me by now.

Nails and Hair . . . Feng Shui Or Be Square

I've been in a bit of a funk lately—sort of blah and looking all droopy like the jaded remnants of once promising tomato plants in our little burned up garden. The speediest glance in the mirror is painful.

It's the heat, I told myself. Bound to be the heat. Got to be the heat.

Well, it's not.

I just happened to chance upon the obvious explanation for my low energy, pitiful-looking self, and it's not the heat. It's the head.

The whole problem, I've discovered, is my hair.

Seems an ancient Chinese philosophy that your surroundings affect your well-being is now addressing the dilemma of bad hair days.

Feng shui, it's called. I pronounce it "fing shoe," even though my friend Beverly tells me that's wrong. But I can't write what she said, so "fing shoe" it's going to be in my limited lingo.

Formerly the domain of home decorators and landscape architects, feng shui has now taken over many of the beauty shops in Southern California.

It's true. You can read about it in the newspaper under *"Tresses and Phenomena."*

Billy Yamaguchi is the feng shui hair pioneer in California. Owner of six salons, he advises folks all about how their hair can totally throw their "chi" or personal energy into chaos.

Out of whack.

Higgeldy-piggeldy.

Plum nasty.

Donna's done my hair for years and I love her. My bad hair is not her fault—I look great when I leave the beauty shop. But in between cuts I'm prone to shower, towel my head, and go. Anything more is too much trouble.

I was in the shop the other day and asked Donna about feng shui. She said it sounded to her like some kind of oriental Birkenstock.

So I had to explain all about how, as caretaker of my locks, she needs to decide if I'm a fire, earth, metal, water, or wood person. Then she should choose a simple hairstyle that enhances or harmonizes with my fire, earth, metal, water, or wooden personality.

If she could arrange it, I told her, I believe I'd rather be fire than any of the others. Metal is cold and hard; earth and water are too common. And wood? Just a little bit scrubby, I think. Buggy, even.

Donna said fire is good. Every middle-aged woman could do with a little fire every now and then, she declared, but she still wasn't convinced feng shui could get "a head" here in Mississippi.

Why not? For heaven's sake, some of those California beauty shops are charging up to $250 for a feng shui consultation. Donna could get rich quick, I insisted.

She kept combing.

Well then, hey, I'll just consult with Bonnie, my nail person.

See, not only hair is involved here. Folks like Julia Roberts and Drew Barrymore have also had their nails feng-shuied, and I really like the idea of putting the mumbo jumbo on my fingernails.

Picture this. I'm walking down the street and a mugger confronts me with a threatening scowl. I assume a slick karate kid position—feet planted, head thrown back, arms extended, fingers in his face.

"Yiiiiiiiiiiiiiii!" I shrill. "Get thee to thine hidey-hole or I shall scratch out thine eyes with my fiery fearsome freshly feng-shuied fingernails!"

I'm willing to bet he'll turn and skadoot, feng shui shooed, before he can even appreciate that my hair is also feng-shuied, which is a darn shame if I've been able to bring Donna around, spending $250 to get the locks just right.

Oh, well, you win some, you lose some.

Ode To Butterbeans

Hubby G-Man walked in the back door the other day with a huge bag of butterbeans—picked, shelled, washed, and ready for the fatback. I was singing alleluias to our benefactor whose initials are HM, but that's all I'll reveal because the good man might get harassed due to his not spreading the bounty far and wide.

Gloat? Yeah, and it feels good.

One reason gloating feels good is because I remember well the torture involved in picking tasty little butterbeans.

As a matter of fact, the other night after choir practice I literally tippy-toed out of the church when I heard my pals Beverly and Paul and David talking about how the butterbeans were getting plump and anybody who wanted some should bring a bucket and come on to the garden.

Why did I slip out? Because I hate pain, that's why.

Here's the background. David and Paul have gorgeous gardens with bumper crops. These two guys definitely have cucumber-green thumbs, and they love to share. Well, last year about this time David announced to us choristers that the butterbeans were ready for picking and we could all fill up our freezers. Who, he asked, wanted some?

My vocal cords kicked in before my brain did. I hollered, "Me!"—a misspeak that resulted in my having to drag out of bed the next morning and trot my sleepy self out to the garden.

But the awful picking was not without reward. I did end up with a nice pot of butterbeans, and also wrote a poem about the experience which I actually was able to get published in a small North Carolina literary journal of "accessible Southern fiction and poetry." (That means no big words or high-falutin' ideas.)

The poem is called:

ODE TO BUTTERBEANS

Absolutely's what I told him
when he asked me if I wanted
to pick purple butterbeans
before he gave them all away.
I arose before the rooster
could announce it was the dawning
of another steamy, humid-horrid
Mississippi day.
I slipped into jeans which hadn't
in their whole lives seen a bean plant
and a tee-shirt of my daughter's
that proclaimed, "I Shop eBay."
Then I headed for the garden,
a real bean abundant garden,
and I spent two hours picking
in the muddy, gummy clay.
As the perspiration clouded
my already dreadful vision,
I picked butterbeans and wondered
if my brain were near decay.
See, I couldn't help but ponder
as the sun began to bake me
how for two bucks at the market
I could have a bean heyday.
But there's something about picking
and the shelling that makes eating
really lovely— 'specially after
aching muscles get okay.
Absolutely's what I told him
when he asked me if my bounty,
those most glorious beans of purple,
graced my suppertime buffet.
After two long hours picking,
then another hour shelling,
I was proud to get one heaping pot of
butterbeans gourmet.

(Can you tell I don't know beans when it comes to writing poetry? NOTE TO HM: You keep bringing the beans; I'll avoid the picking, the poems, and the pitiful puns.)

Ohhhh, Tannenbaum . . .

I don't know how other families manage their holidays, but we've worked out a system where we share Christmases with our children's inlaws—one year here, the next year there. This works out well, giving hubby G-Man and me a boisterous, rollicking celebration—then around seven hundred days to get over it.

During our off years (and this year is one of those), G-Man and I usually avoid the depressing situation of sitting at home alone on Christmas Day by going to THEIR homes or taking a short trip. No fun celebrating Christmas in an empty house.

We're used to Christmases past, when our four (Emily, Bethany, Will, and Tom) would wake at the crack of dawn, pester their daddy and me till we slid out of bed, then drag us to the towering Christmas tree in the den to see what Santa had left.

During our off-year holiday season, however, I still must decorate, just as if the house is going to be filled with children and dogs and cats and things live other than the hub and me.

I've hosted the Christmas party for women in my church for eons now, missing only a few years due to a broken ankle, an unavoidable trip or two, and a sick daughter. The church ladies expect me to haul out the holly and candles, and I do. In abundance.

And of course, there must be a tree.

Last week I brought down the boxes of ornaments from the attic and began the happy task of decorating this season's grand tannenbaum, a little four foot, prelighted artificial creation from Wally's World. (Well, as an aunt once said, "It's the EFFECT you're going for.")

There I was, digging through the first box, pulling out the most wonderful, tattered, beloved ornaments any family could have collected over thirty-something years, and I began to cry.

I wasn't sobbing or blubbering—just mopping tears from my eyes and cheeks, examining the ornaments, sighing, wondering where the years have gone.

None of the ornaments are fine. Some are slightly damaged and all are worn from years of gracing our tree. And all are special.

I placed on our glorious tree: macaroni angels made by David and Kathleen Schubert; a couple of beautiful German ornaments from Carol Tatum; a jolly, fat wooden Santa from Floyd and Molly Shaman, circa 1992; crocheted balls from my Czech friend, Ludmila Vopatova, and crocheted snowflakes from Vera Eckert; needlepoint ornaments from Jackie Mitchell and from Ann and Rusty Ruscoe (mid 70s, I think); a tiny MSU cowbell given us at Jason and Delina Horton's December wedding several years ago; a painted dough angel with these words on the back: "To Ms. Beth from St. Luke 3rd and 4th graders, 1994."

An almost mutilated red plaid horsie, one leg chewed off by Cupid, our family dog in the mid-70s, found his place of honor on this 2002 higgledy-piggledy tree. Then there were hand-painted glass balls from Beverly Jacks and a small Santa fashioned from dough by Nan Sanders.

A holly topped bell, painted by Peggy Matthews, with "Merry Christmas, 1982" brought back wonderful memories, as did the pretty blue angel for the top of the tree—given to Bethany years ago by Melissa Norquist.

Then I got to the "Children's Box." I picked up a little brass Christmas tree with Will's fourth grade school picture in the center, hung it carefully on a branch, then reached for one of Tom's treasured baseball ornaments. Next came a wee blond angel—I always bought blond angels for Emily each year—and a dark-haired cheerleader complete with pom poms (made by Janice Arnold, I think) that was Bethany's.

There were more. My tears continued to spill as each ornament reminded me of wonderful family Christmases with the merry laughter of children filling the house.

Oh, I'm OK now—still sentimental, but the tears are dried. And, don't you worry, taking inspiration from many area football fans, I'm quite comfy with this thought:

"Just wait till NEXT year!"

Old Friendships Chase The Blues Away

"Are we going to be friends forever?" asked Piglet.
"Even longer," Pooh answered.

— A. A. Milne

The weekend began in a most inauspicious manner when I found myself locked in the garage.

No, my physical self was not locked in such tight quarters—my vehicle was. The automatic garage door at daughter Emily's home in Mobile decided to open only partially. This was frustrating because I was due in Jackson, Mississippi, that afternoon to participate in festivities surrounding the wedding of a friend's son.

Fuming, I pulled and tugged and threatened savage vengeance, but no luck. Finally I called a garage door repairman who came and worked his hocus pocus. Cost me one hundred bucks to get out of the garage.

Also, wrestling with the dumb door mechanism cost me more than a C-note. I was left with two broken fingernails to complement the busted toenail I'd suffered earlier after a can of frozen orange juice concentrate fell on my tootsie. I'd had no time to shower and had grabbed the top layer of clothing on a bedroom chair to throw on my body that morning as I awaited the repairman with his trusty garage door tools.

No question, I looked like the last rose of summer, and I was heading to Jackson to reunite with six childhood friends for this wedding—friends for whom I really wanted to look smashing. This girl was not happy.

Fortunately, arriving in Jackson before the others, I was able to bathe and repair the fingernails, but the toe remained a mess. The first girlfriend on the scene assured me nobody would notice. "They will not be gathering in corners to discuss your big toe," she said.

To be sure, there was nowhere to go but up with this weekend, and I'm happy to report that is exactly what happened.

The other girls arrived amid much hugging and squealing, and we added two pals of our wedding hostess to round out the group. (What better for a crew of women reconnecting with their silly centers than to have an audience?)

So we lounged, downing cashews and chocolate chip cookies and anything edible within reach. We chatted at length, screaming with laughter at our jokes and stories.

We had lots of years to cover. The seven of us could boast of a dozen husbands, 20 kids, a stack of graduate degrees, and a crazy array of odd twists and turns in our lives.

"Yeah," said T, who's been single for several years following her third divorce. "I used to have a little black book with pages of men's names and phone numbers. Now I have a list of my doctors and pharmacies."

"Let's not discuss our aches and pains, including husbands," said S. "Tell us about your kids, M."

"Well, my son sells monkeys and other exotic animals," began M. "Recently he had a deformed camel. The hump was bad because the camel was malnourished in infancy and he was going to require a special saddle—not to mention his snout was crooked. So my son wasn't sure he could sell this animal, but he did. A lady in Dallas bought the camel and taught him to catch a Frisbee."

We looked at her.

"Well," W spoke finally, "I WAS going to say that my son is a dentist, but nevermind."

We nodded. How can you best a son who sells a crooked-mouthed, hump-deprived, Frisbee-catching camel?

To make a short story even longer, the wedding/reunion weekend was positively grand. The bride and groom were elegant, the ceremony was lovely, and the reception was a hoo-hah-hah affair with music by the "Gents." We girls danced wildly together till our feet "swoled up" big as douche bags.

Benjamin Disraeli is quoted as saying there's magic in childhood friendships. "They soften the heart," he wrote. And, oh, how often we let these friendships slip away.

I'm determined not to let so many years go by before we old friends get together again. Gurus in medical circles all maintain that making merry is important for our health and sanity.

And reunions are good therapy—safe times to cry and threaten and fuss about those significant others. ("Really, y'all, how do you get over your first love?" asked M. "You marry him," said T, as we all fell out in convulsions of laughter.)

I pulled away from the hotel early Sunday morning, reflecting on how the weekend had blessed me with the blithest of spirits—even as I faced a long drive home. A simple reunion of a few old pals can chase far, far away the blues of everyday life, contrary garage doors and, yeah, even broken nails.

Let's hear it for the girlfriends!

Organizing My Chaos

Amidst the rubble I call a home office, I sit at the computer, about to launch into yet another Snippets column for the literary world. The weekly deadline is approaching and I'm stressed. Scanning my "Idea Notebook," I see where I've jotted: "Five Habits That Annoy Women," "Fat Gene Discovered," "Will J-Lo Marry Ben?"

My brain responds: "No" and "No" and "Who's J-Lo?"

About that time the computer dinger goes "bing," which tells me I have an e-mail message. This is usually advertising spam, bothersome when I'm trying to come up with a subject for Snippets, but at the moment I'm column-stumped and feel like procrastinating, so I go to my e-mail box.

There I find a message, sent to me and five hundred other folks, from my friend Kevin. He informs us he's updating his computer address book and needs our current snailmail addresses.

This sets me to wondering how many people still send snailmail and how in the sam hill anybody has time to update a computer address book.

But I send the address to him because I know that, like his sweet mama, he might remember my birthday in January with a cute card or something.

The address wings its way through cyberspace while my incredulity lingers. Why is it that Kevin, a highly motivated, organized fellow, has time to update his computer address book while I hardly have time to enjoy a good sneeze?

I think about Kevin and experience an AHA! moment.

Organized. The man's organized. That's the key.

Yep. Coming up with a column idea would be so much easier if I had a neat, orderly office and life.

A couple of weeks ago I went to a beautiful morning coffee at the outta-sight home of Cindy S. You've got to see this house to believe it.

Not a comb on a counter. Not a brown tip on a peace lily. Not a dust mite in the manor. We guests all peeped in Cindy's closets, and they were immaculate too. Didn't check her medicine cabinets, but I 'spect the little bottles are in alphabetical order.

I asked my pals when we left the party, "Where in the world does she keep her old newspapers and magazines?"

"She doesn't collect junk," said Beverly. "She pitches it."

"Yeah," I said, "but you go and pitch good junk, and that's the very thing you need two months later."

Two months later, of course, if you're like me, you've kept the stuff but you can't find it 'cause your chaos is not organized.

So, I'm staring at my computer, unable to come up with a single idea for Snippets. Instead I'm thinking about how disorganized I am and how I suffer from Disposophobia, and I remember a tale about two brothers, hermits from somewhere up in the East, whose dead bodies had to be unearthed from 136 tons of mess before they could be removed from their junk packed house.

One of the brothers, Homer, was an invalid, see, and the other, Langley, would grope his way through a network of tunnels carved out in the mountains of junk to get to Homer.

Alas, one day a pile of heavy stuff fell on Langley, crushing him, and then poor Homer starved to death, sitting in his chair, surrounded by piles of important objects like the insides of pianos and old encyclopedias and Model-T engines and medical specimens in glass jars.

I glance around my office. I see newspapers and books and bunches of pictures and catalogues, an old typewriter with no ribbon, and sticky notes all over the place—nothing, I figure, that would bang me up too bad if it fell on my head, but most certainly a classic display of disorganization.

I sigh and realize there's no way I can write a column today. My thoughts are too scattered. But I've got more ideas on scraps of paper somewhere on this cluttered desk.

I know I jotted something down about a new magazine just out called "Balance." It's guaranteed to help readers get their lives in order.

Another magazine subscription is just what I need. Another stack of stuff.

Sounds like a Snippets column to me.

Pajama Trivia

Not since Little Red Riding Hood caught the big, bad wolf under the duvet wearing Granny's jammies have nightclothes been so exciting.

I say this because of a teency-weency newspaper article last week that proclaimed to the fashion world that nightgowns and pajamas are now the "in" thing to wear to the grocery store and to yon shopping mall stall over there in Shanghai.

"Shoppers wearing pajamas or nightgowns haggle with fishmongers or look over the goods at the stalls of vegetable peddlers," the article stated.

"It's a common sight in China's biggest, most prosperous city: men and women in public dressed as if in the intimacy of their bedrooms."

"Oooh, la la," as the French might say. How unusual to see la negligee in la marketplace.

Normally, I wouldn't have given this titillating bit of information a second glance, but then I began to think about how comfy a baggy pair of jammies would be for us Southerners and how easy it would be to throw those suckers in the washing machine after a sweaty shopping spree.

Shanghainese may be on to something here.

Actually, and I'll bet you didn't know this, nightclothes were first fashioned in the 1500s. Up until then people either slept naked or in their day clothes. I didn't learn this from reading *"Lady Chatterly's Lover,"* I promise. Fact is, if I run up on wacky information, I enjoy researching the topic further. That's how I know this naked/day clothes trivia.

I also found out that during World War II Winston Churchill often stayed in his pajamas all morning, reading newspapers, dictating letters and memos, going over secret papers and documents. He usually bathed and dressed around 1 p.m., then proceeded with the more formal part of his day: meetings, visits, speeches, and so forth. At 6 p.m. Churchill undressed, put on his nightclothes and had an hour sleep. After waking and getting dressed once more, he ate and worked till the wee hours of the morn, at which time he got back in his pajamas and retired for the night.

Fascinating, yes? I'm just wondering if the man put the same pajamas on, then off, then on, then off—not that this is something I really should wonder. It's just that I'm concerned about all the washing his wife had to do. Fabric, however, was at a premium in Britain during World War II, so I'm assuming he recycled. Surely . . .

Unless he was like the poor youngster in a certain pre-school class here 'bouts who asked his teacher for help. The child needed a bathroom break, you see, but, alas, he was wearing a pair of baggy drawers, pajama-like, with a drawstring waist. The drawstring was knotted. And tangled. And impossible to loosen.

The teacher worked valiantly, but to no avail. The string was hopelessly entwined, and, well, you can guess the rest of the story.

And is there a moral to the poor preschooler's nasty tail, uh, tale?

Just this: If you decide to wear your jammies to work, to school, to the grocery store or to schmooze with vegetable peddlers, be sure to choose ones with elastic waistbands.

Think about it. Tangled strings could affect the whole course of history. If, for example, Winston had been unable to get his strings untwisted, an over-worked Mrs. Churchill would surely have done him in.

So, folks, spread the word: Nightclothes are in for going out.

Look for me. I'll be the one haggling with fishmongers in my red flannel nightie and wool socks. Hubba hubba.

Right To Bare Arms

Oh, yikers. It's that terrible time of year again. You know, the season of our (sleeveless) discontent.

This is the time when cute young things wear tank tops and halters to places like baseball games and grocery stores just to antagonize us jacketed older girls with gelatinous triceps.

I'd like to tell those darlings their time is coming, but maybe it won't.

I say that because I live next door to Susan W., who is not exactly a young chick—but she looks like one. Disgusting.

Every morning I slowly slide from my bed and stagger to the kitchen to turn the coffeemaker on. And what's the first thing I see when I look out the window? The green SUV of Susan's walking/fitness partner, another mature cutie, Jo P. These girls walk every morning, rain or shine, war or peace, in the heat of summer or in winter's chill. They are out the door before the sun's up, and they leave that blame green SUV of Jo's parked on the street in front of my kitchen window, mocking me, calling my attention to the fact that I'm out of breath just reaching for my coffee mug.

I get on exercise kicks every few months because I know I should. I want to look like Susan and Jo and the teens at the ballpark, I really do, but here's my philosophy. I've read that for every minute we exercise, we add a minute to our lives. Add it up. I figure that exercising right now will give me an extra five months to live in a retirement or nursing home when I'm on up into the elder years, which will run me from $3000 to $5000 a month. This is good?

I guess I would die healthier.

My friend Kitty went to a doctor to get help with weight loss. He told her just to eat regularly for two days, then skip a day, and repeat this schedule for two weeks. He promised her she'd lose at least five or ten pounds.

Kitty went back to see him two weeks later and proudly showed off her new figure—she'd shed nearly fifteen pounds. The doctor was amazed. But

Kitty told him she almost dropped dead that third day.

"From hunger?" the doctor said.

"Nope," said Kitty, "from skipping."

Exercise will do that—eliminate the pounds and kill you, all at the same time.

Anyway, I'm in shape. Round is a shape.

Hubby G-Man and I have a treadmill which has served at different times as a clothes rack, a magazine holder, and an object of interest for toddling grandkids. I give it a go every week or so to keep it from completely rusting away, and I truly do enjoy the workout because it's nice to hear heavy breathing again. (I didn't make that up. I read it somewhere and got a chuckle.)

But the treadmill really doesn't help our upper bodies that much.

Never fear. I've discovered the perfect exercise. This is ideal for toning, firming, sculpting and defining flabby arms and shoulders, which most everybody has but Susan, Jo, and the Tank Top Tammies.

The exercise guru who described the procedure instructed as follows:

"Get a five pound potato sack for each hand. Holding the sacks, extend your arms straight out at your sides and hold them there as long as you can. The next week, move up to ten pound potato sacks, then fifty pound potato sacks, then finally one hundred pound potato sacks. Work up to where you can hold those sacks out for several minutes at a time.

"Eventually you can put a few potatoes in the sacks, but don't overdo it."

I hope Susan and Jo read this. They could probably benefit from this potato sack exercise.

Me? I'm just gonna put the sacks right smack over my head and go on with my bad self.

Sigmund Freud, Please Phone Home

I have a notion there are readers out there who would like for me to write about somebody other than hubby G-Man every now and then. I honestly try, but the man continues to give me rich material with which to work—even when he's sleeping.

Always after a good night's snooze, G-man and I awake, and this is how it goes: He stretches and laughs, and I yawn and say, "OK. Tell me about your dream."

I'm not sure what goes on in G-Man's subconscious during his nocturnal flights of fancy, but I can tell you this: The guy has one wacko cinema reeling in his head throughout the night.

Well, I've debated and debated whether to write about a really special dream he had several weeks ago. I decided NO, then changed my mind, then decided NO once more. But the dream's bizarre images wouldn't go away.

G-Man's early morning description of this particular dream so fascinated me that I've not been able to let go of it. What was the meaning of the symbolism therein? How does one explain the mysterious sub-cortical thoughts that obviously had my dear husband's mind a muddle? Mr. Freud, where are you when we need you?

Well, by crackity, I'm guessing Snippets readers are all up into dream interpretation, and I figure I'll get comments from my readers—maybe all fifteen of them. Any assistance is appreciated, as this could be crucial for the future of G-Man's and my relationship. Here's the dream:

As he slept, G-Man rambled around (in his head, of course) in a big house with many rooms. As he rambled he suddenly noticed there was a huge blister on his arm—a really big, mama-jama-tumor-thing sitting on his elbow. So, after feeling around on this puffy protuberance for a minute, he punctured it with the tines of a fork.

As you might imagine, an effusion of stuff began to gush from the punctured blister.

Now before you dream interpreters start in on this, you must hear the rest of the story, for the efflux is far from run-of-the-mill. Streaming from four tiny holes, much to G-Man's amazement, was a flow of onions and gravy.

He was so captivated with this unusual sight that he ran to another room to find an empty toothpaste tube. He unscrewed the cap and began to try to suck the onions and gravy into the tube. This was a difficult task, and he didn't finish before the alarm clock awoke him. And then it was that he began to share his interesting vision with me.

Attempting to help him figure all this out, I went online to a site that promised to help visitors interpret dreams. The instructions said: "In the boxes below, please enter three important words or symbols from your dream. We will then give you an interpretation."

So I did.

In the first box I typed "onions." In the second box I typed "gravy." I finally settled on "blister" for the third box because that was the way G-Man described his bump.

You know what? The folks sitting on the other end of my computer wires had no clue. They sent their interpretation back totally blank.

What to do? Maybe, I thought, I've got the third blank wrong. I deleted "blister" and typed "toothpaste tube."

Still no interpretation.

Whoa boy, we'd flat stumped those suckers. I mean, here were skilled dream interpreters who could cover symbols all the way from aardvarks to zymometers, and they'd never dealt with onions and gravy and toothpaste tubes before.

So much for the so-called authorities.

I'm willing to bet I get valid explanations from several of my Snippets readers. The best interpretation gets a prize. I haven't decided what the prize should be, but I'm leaning toward a free meal at a good Southern cafe—maybe a big thick hamburger steak smothered with . . . naaaa.

Sixth Avenue Peddlers

My sister Kathy and I always liked to sell things. Back in the mid-50s when we were younglings, she and I sold anything we could get our hands on so we could buy Baby Ruths and Eskimo Pies over at Hilburn's Store.

We sold lemonade, of course, from makeshift stands next to the street, but most of our dealings were much more creative: corsages made from mimosa blossoms, plastic beads strung on wire for earrings, homemade hotpads, jars of tadpoles.

We were busy.

Our most ambitious business endeavor took place the summer of 1955. I'd just finished 5th grade, Kathy had finished 4th grade, and the summer stretched before us like one long money-making opportunity.

That's when I saw the ad in a Photoplay magazine.

For only twenty bucks we could order a huge supply of Christmas cards—probably four or five dozen boxes. Maybe six. Then we could sell the 10-card boxes for fifty cents and the 20-card boxes for a dollar.

Brainy me did the math fast. All we had to do was sell the whole stash of Christmas cards and we'd be rolling in dough. We'd be able to buy enough Double Bubble to last till Halloween.

So I begged Daddy for twenty dollars, couldn't believe my luck when he gave it to me, filled out the form, stuck the twenty dollar bill in the envelope, and sent the order on its way to Happy Holiday Greetings.

Long about the first of July the shipment arrived, and, cross my heart, the cards were knock-out.

There were boxes of Ho Ho Ho funny cards and boxes of "For unto us . . ." religious cards. There were white-on-white angel cards. There were Norman Rockwells and Ye Olde Homesteads. There were red birds and gold balls and green hollies and just any kind of Christmas card a soul could desire.

Granted, the Christmas season was a bit in the future that hot July day, but

Kak and I were raring to go.

We set up shop on the screened porch of our house there on Sixth Avenue.

I found a nice photo case in the bottom of Mama's chest, emptied the old pictures, and had us a dandy money holder. I had paper to record the sales. I had pencils. I had a comfy chair and a ceiling fan sending nice breezes my way . . . and Kathy was assigned sales duty.

This was only fair since I'd done all the leg-work for our business venture. I'd secured the financing, I'd done the paperwork, I'd set up our office, and I'd even torn open the big box—no easy task.

Kathy trudged off down the street dragging the bulky box of Christmas cards behind her. This was no easy task either, I admit, for at that time Sixth Avenue was not paved, just sprayed every summer with some kind of sticky ole tar stuff. But Kathy was dutiful and understood the importance of team-work, so off she went, sweating like a horse, pulling that box through the tar.

Now, I ask you, who would have the heart to turn down a perspiring child selling Christmas cards in the middle of July? Most all the women in a six block area were dears, and Kathy sold those Christmas cards like hotcakes.

She'd sell a bunch, then bring the wad of money back to me. I'd count it. Record it. Let her get a drink of water. Send her out again.

Well, toward the end of that first sales day I saw her coming back toward the house, the big cardboard box bumping and thumping through the tarred gravel.

She jerked the box up the steps, slammed the screened door, handed me the money, and said, "I'm not doing this tomorrow."

"You got to," I said. "You're the salesman."

"Yeah, but it's too hot. And anyway, I've sold to everybody I can sell to."

"Did you try Louise Warner?"

"Yep. That's her five dollar bill for five angel boxes."

"Did you go to Rita Bizzell's?"

"Yep. Her money's in there too."

"What about Mrs. Wutzername?"

"Nope. Mrs. Wutzername didn't want a single box—just kept hanging her wash on the line and said, 'For crying out loud, this is the middle of July!'"

"What?" I was shocked. "I know good and well she didn't say that."

"Well, she didn't want any, and I'm not doing this tomorrow."

One thing about Kathy, when she makes up her mind there's no budging her. Anyway, I was exhausted from sitting on that porch all day.

We paid Daddy back his twenty dollars and had about five left over—two for Kak and three for me. And, thanks to Mrs. Wutzername, Mama had a gracious plenty Christmas cards for years and years to come.

So, everything turned out just fine. Couldn't have planned it better if I'd had a MBA.

But then, with our pal Judy's covert assistance, we went and sold her daddy's honest to goodness ivory dominoes and got whippings with a limb from the privet hedge.

Trying to thwart free enterprise, the grownups were, but we fixed them. Wasn't long before we switched from selling to buying—charm bracelets and Elvis records and tube after tube of Clearasil.

Frankly, I don't think those ladies really wanted to buy our Christmas cards in the first place.

Tadpoles either.

Sleep Research Answers Questions

There's hardly a topic more fascinating than sleep. Many scientists are presently investigating the subject with lots of experiments. Lots of why, wherefore, and whences.

So I have decided to share with readers everything I've learned about sleep. I know a lot. I have boocoodles of first hand experience, and I read sleep related articles all the time.

How come?

Well, I live with a tossing, turning, speechifying dynamo of a husband whom I affectionately call G-Man. I study every tidbit of sleep info I can get my hands on in order to understand this man's nocturnal habits.

Does anyone else live with a spouse who talks incessantly while sleeping? I'll match mine with yours. I do believe G-Man was verbal even in the womb. He never hushes. Never. Sometimes he jabbers all night long.

Consumed with paranoia as I age, I've begun to wonder if his sleep talking has anything to do with me.

For example, the other night as he slept he kept talking about what nice folks the Icebergs are. Icebergs? He's lying in bed with me and he's thinking down deep in his subconscious la-la-land about icebergs?

I don't want to interpret that.

I do know that counselors have advised husbands to talk in their sleep if they really want their wives to listen. Ummm . . . I will admit that sometimes G-Man tells me things that whoosh in one ear and out the other.

But not when he's sleeping.

When he's sleeping and talking he's got my undivided attention—like the other night I was telling you about. We'd been asleep (or semi-) for over an hour.

"The Icebergs are such nice folks," he ups and says, as his brain functions somewhere between "hello" and "beeeeeeep."

I roll over and say, "The who?"

"The Icebergs. Dr. and Mrs. Iceberg."

And I say, "Uhhh . . . where did you meet the nice Icebergs?"

Then he mumbles something I can't understand, so I press on.

"Tell me about Mrs. Iceberg. Is she attractive?"

"Yeah," he says, so I go for more.

This can continue for thirty minutes or longer, and the man never wakes up. I could be the wimpiest enemy interrogator on this earth and G-Man would tell me everything I want to know before sun-up.

Actually, I'm now discovering from big-time researchers that even when G-Man's not sleep talking I can possibly still find out all sorts of things about him just by staring at him in the night.

Have you heard? A Reuters press release has described common sleep positions and what they reveal about our personality traits. For example:

* 51% of women prefer the fetal sleeping position, indicating shyness and sensitivity.

* Those snoozers who lie flat on their backs with arms at their sides in the soldier position are normally quiet and reserved.

* Sleep on your side with legs outstretched and arms down? You have a social, easy-going personality.

* What about the freefall position, flat on your tummy? You're in the minority. Only about 6.5% of sleepers do this. You're brash and gregarious.

Unfortunately, when I stare at G-Man in the night, his position is never the same. But he's a lawyer and you know what that means. Sometimes they lie one way, and sometimes they lie another way.

Sleep position, however, is not the only slumber related topic being discussed in the news right now. Another newspaper article the other day discussed our "circadian clocks," which sounds to me like something to do with grasshoppers.

But no, circadian clocks are actually rhythms governing our sleep and wake times. And luckily for us humans, we share a weird kind of gene that's vital to this daily cycle with (ta DA!) fruit flies.

Mess up the fruit flies' special circadian clock genes and they die. Just like that. Pssssst. Gone. Off to the big freeze.

Researchers say there's a message here for us humans but I can't figure what it is unless maybe it has to do with Dr. and Mrs. Iceberg.

I'll ask G-Man tonight.

Socking It To The Airlines

I thought I had suffered ultimate humiliation when a grouchy guard at the Memphis airport several weeks ago instructed me to take off my shoes.

Why?

Well, I don't spend money on socks. The pair I was wearing were the worst, the very worst, in my dresser drawer. Should you need to define "threadbare," just visualize these socks. I had a tiny hole where my left big toe peeped through, and each little thread in the heels of both clung to the others in a most tenacious manner, as if to say, "Hey, buddies, perhaps we could remain knitted one more day and then let's sprrrrong—give it up."

When I heard "Step over here, ma'am, and take your shoes off," I immediately began to anticipate the reaction of the crowd stacked behind me. Tittering and pointing were bound to turn my red face even redder. I could imagine the whispers.

"Look at her pitiful socks. Good grief! Y'all want to pitch in a quarter each to get the woman a pair of decent socks?"

I'm sorry. Socks are just NOT on my "To Get" list. But after that embarrassing episode, then and there, I vowed a sock-it-to-me spectacle at the airport with my footsies should never happen again. That's right. When I returned home I went and bought a half dozen thick pair just to wear in airports.

But there's no rest for the weary in this world. I soon discovered I've got a flying impediment much more serious with which to deal.

I'm sure I wasn't the only "flier-when-there's-absolutely-no-other-way-to-get-there" who recoiled at a recent news release recently put out by the Associated Press. I opened the newspaper and retched as I read: "Now you have to weigh in before you fly."

For real? This is a joke, right?

Would that it were. The Federal Aviation Administration is announcing this passenger weigh-in policy for small commuter and regional planes, trying to determine whether current weight estimates are accurate.

Don't want to get on the scales? Well, honey, you don't go.

The whole problem has to do with aerodynamics: weight, lift, thrust and drag. Lift has to equal weight, and when it doesn't, the plane can't fly. In plain speak, if the amount of lift drops below the weight of the airplane, the plane will, uh, descend rapidly or maybe never even get off the ground.

I thought it interesting that the airport folks are given the option of asking passengers their weight, rather than making us weigh in on the scales. Here's the kicker though: if you tell them you weigh, say, 140 pounds, they have the right to add 10 pounds to whatever you tell them because most people lie.

C'mon, now. I'd never lie about my weight (she says as she watches the heavens for lightning bolts).

And sure, they're starting with the little bitty planes, but you know what's next. Picture this:

I'm set to fly on a 747 because I passed the boarding exam when I lied on my ticket application and said I weighed 125 pounds. The 747 pulls up, all sleek and shiny, 232 feet long, 63 feet high, weighing 435 tons—plenty of space for little 'ole me.

I march to the counter, ID in hand. The weaselly ticket guy suppresses a snicker and says:

"Gooood morning! Step on the scales, plea . . . Oh, yikers, lady, I'm afraid your numbers just won't do."

He smiles benignly while I sniffle.

"You see, ma'am," he says, "we estimate that a typical adult passenger in the wintertime weighs 185 pounds—that's with heavy clothing and carry-ons. I'm afraid with those thick socks you're wearing you exceed our modest estimates by a few eency weency pounds. So sorry. Stay home."

Well, bless Pete, they can take my shoes and confiscate my trusty nail clippers, but there will be no pounds added to this girl because of heavy socks.

Nosirree, if those little sniveling airline agents even mention weight to me, I'll guarantee them some lifting, thrusting, and dragging . . . and it won't be the airplane.

Sparkle Plenty Bombs

My pals who see me every day in bluejeans and sneakers will attest to the fact that I'm certainly not one to advise when it comes to proper stuff—especially fashion or topics like that.

I don't know much, but I do know a little about unimportant things. And since Christmas is right around the corner and men will be putting out big bucks to thrill their sweeties on Christmas morning, I felt I should share what I know so the guys won't make serious mistakes.

I can tell you, for example, that the southern girl who's had a proper upbringing knows a well dressed belle never wears diamonds in the daytime. An engagement ring is okay, but the rest of the glitter is appropriately left for formal events held after the sun goes down.

The reason I bring this up is because I ran into an acquaintance yesterday morning, and honey, she was garlanded and ornamented fit to kill. At the grocery store yet.

As we were discussing whether real ambrosia has nuts or not, the girl was flashing those diamonds in my face. She had sparks on her ears. Sparks on her neck. Sparks on her fingers. Sparks on her wrists. She looked like the Fourth of July.

Remember that baby doll back forty years ago we called Sparkle Plenty? Uh huh.

Anyway, the most dazzling sparkle was reserved for her diamond encrusted watch. Diamond encrusted watch? What's with this? Back in the early '60s, Mrs. Moses and Mrs. Peacock (my eighth grade home economics teachers) insisted, as I've already said, diamonds are NOT to be worn in the daytime. But here's the clincher—watches are NOT to be worn to formal events in the evening. So when, pray tell, is one supposed to wear a diamond encrusted watch?

Never, dear readers.

I'm sure jewelry store folks will say that's a bunch of baloney, but I'm just telling you what I was taught by Mrs. Peacock and Mrs. Moses—who proudly led us junior high gals out of the wilderness of fashion ignorance.

And since I've never had that many diamonds to speak of, I like that "Save-Em-For-The-Ball" rule. I don't go to that many balls either, so I suppose I'm snug as a bug wrapped in my excellent fashion sense.

Which brings me to Shoewels—rhymes with jewels—which is most definitely a bit of fashion I should warn men to avoid. Am I the last person in the whole wide world to find out about Shoewels? I hope not. And don't go telling me Shoewels have been around for twenty years. I'm doing my best to stay young and funky, and frankly, being hip at my age is not that easy.

I saw some Shoewels this past summer in Colorado. They spilled from baskets on a shop counter and filled me with as much pain as a bucket of clip-on earrings. The sign on the counter said, "Let's Get Funky." Okay, I thought, give me a three step program and I'm all for it.

I wasn't all for it though when I discovered that in order to get funky I had to wear those Shoewels on my ankles and toes. Ouch.

Shoppers can get them beaded or braided or bejeweled (surely diamonds are only available for evening wear), and they encircle the ankle as they snake down around your second toe. Buy six pairs to mix and match, and they'll throw in a seventh pair free. Imagine that? A different pair of Shoewels for each day of the week.

May brave souls wear Shoewels with shoes? Of course, the boutique cutie told me. The bead closest to the toe fits above the edge of most pumps. Doesn't take any time to get used to the pressure of tiny little hard things digging into your flesh or bands of gold cutting off the blood supply to your tootsies.

Naaa. I don't think so. My sculptor pal, Floyd Shaman, is carving funky "Mesquite-toes" key chains from a bunch of mesquite wood. I think those will suit me better. But I want my "Mesquite-toes" key chain without diamonds.

I rarely drive at night.

Station Wagons – Cool Again!

Hold on to your bouffants, folks, there is a comeback in the making. I'm not talking about carbohydrates, not talking about "Cherries in the Snow" nail polish, not talking about Bobbie Gentry.

I'm talking about the coolest of the cool: low slung, sporty station wagons.

That's right. Station wagons are back on the scene, and I must say I've missed them sorely. I'm not ashamed to admit I drove a white, chrome encrusted Ford wagon in high school in the early '60s. Not hip, you say? Well, I'll tell you this, that '58 clunker had a great AM radio and held a lot of buddies.

Ten years or so later I was still in a station wagon, a green one, but this time I was doing the young matron thing, hauling children and dogs.

These were the days before car seats and seat belts. My kids and their little friends were often packed in our station wagon like sardines. One day was especially bad. The vehicle was a riot of screamers and kickers, and I was yelling at them over my shoulder from the driver's seat.

"Hush! Behave! Y'all get quiet!"

"But, Mama," hollered one, "we can't be quiet!"

Turns out she had an excellent point.

"Why?" I screamed.

"Because you're squashing Jim's head in the window!"

I hit the brakes. Upon release from his incarcerated state, Jim squalled but was otherwise fine.

Excuse me, but it's a long way from the driver's seat to the back of a station wagon. How was I to know the boy had his head poked out the window as I pressed the "roll me up" button with one hand and massaged my throbbing brow with the other?

I was shaken, wavering in my devotion to station wagons with automatic windows in the waaay back. Anyway, the first gasoline crunch happened long about then and we decided to trade for something more economical.

Then American car makers began to produce fewer and fewer wagons. Eventually (she explains, guiltily) we ignored gas concerns and moved on to mini-vans, followed by SUVs. We've driven the gamut in our household, throwing in a traditional automobile and pick-up every now and then for variety.

So why am I gleeful over the station wagon comeback?

First of all, climbing up into an SUV is getting trickier and trickier. Disembarking is worse—sort of like rappelling Kilimanjaro. And mini-vans? Naaa. I backed into too many telephone poles. Besides, I'm a clutterer, and vans are magnets for clutter.

Why not a regular ol' car? I'm on the highway a lot and need something sturdier. In the event of a crash, I'd rather be on top.

I chatted the other day with my car dealer friend Edward, and he said automobile makers are shying away from actually calling the new station wagons by that name. They're not station wagons, they're Chrysler Pacificas or whatever their snazzy names are.

He says these vehicles are hybrid, a cross between an SUV and a van, just an oversized station wagon.

Station wagon? Weird name. Where does that name come from anyway? I looked it up.

The very first station wagons back in the early 1900s were "depot hacks," used primarily around train stations to transport passengers and luggage. These were "wagons" used at railway "stations." Get it?

Station wagon popularity spread over the next few years until their Golden Age—1955 to 1975. Uh huh, my hauling days fit squarely in those two decades.

Hey, this Baby Boomer is all into nostalgia, and station wagons afford plenty of that. Maybe they're not the most elegant ride, but if John Lennon could drive a wagon, I reckon I can too.

Put me lower to the ground, give me seats I can reach across, and paint me up in vivid mustard with a bold grill, plenty of luggage room, and maybe just a tinge of retro styling. I'll be happy.

Oh yeah, I mustn't forget one last feature. Your friendly car thieves don't want station wagons.

According to the Highway Loss Data Institute, most thieves will pass your wagon by for something classier.

We should all be so cool.

Tennis and Good Ole Boys

I always get a hankering when the weather turns pretty to venture out onto the tennis courts with the sunshine and breezes, the cute outfits, the healthy glow of perspiration glistening on rosy cheeks, and the bap-bap-bap of the ball as the volley whizzes back and forth, back and forth, back and . . . well, sometimes forth.

The hankering lasts all of, oh, five seconds usually before I come to my senses; nevertheless, I do miss being involved in athletics—especially tennis because it's just so downright civilized.

I also like to read about tennis stars in the sports section of the newspaper. I know all about their strengths and weaknesses, their temper tantrums, their backgrounds, and the big bucks they get for hitting that little ball so hard and so well.

Yep, I stay on top of the goings-on in the world of tennis.

But not hubby G-Man. He is tennis ignorant.

Summer before last we were in Las Vegas helping our friends, David and Paula, get remarried—a renewing of vows in a most celebratory and fabulous fashion. G-Man was actually going to "remarry" the couple, and I was to trip the light fantastic with my agile fingers on the organ keys there in the chapel of the Las Vegas Grand Casino.

This was my first trip to Las Vegas ever in my whole long life, and I was taking in all the glitter with a tad of culture shock.

My pal Pat and I walked up to the check-in counter there in the hotel and were greeted by a nice older fellow with a flashy gold name tag on his pocket. I don't remember the man's first name, but the last name was AGASSI.

Hmmm, I thought. The great tennis star, André Agassi, is from Las Vegas. Could this be his father?

"Uh, sir," I said, "would you happen to be kin to André Agassi?"

He beamed. "Yes, indeed," he said, "André is my son."

"I'll bet you're glad he broke up with Brooke Shields, aren't you?" said Pat, smiling her pert little head off.

We were both tickled to death.

Meeting somebody famous—well, famous by association. That was close enough.

Hooo-boy!

Mr. Agassi acknowledged that yes, he was certainly glad André had moved on with his love life.

About that time, G-Man walked up.

"Honey!" I said, mega star struck, but maintaining my usual mature demeanor. "This is André Agassi's father!"

Unfortunately, sometimes G-Man doesn't pay enough attention to what I'm saying—and his eyesight certainly isn't what it used to be.

He glanced at Mr. Agassi's name tag and told me later he thought the tag said Allegrezza, one of the Mississippi Delta's fine families.

And then, his southern accent ringing through that Las Vegas lobby as he reached across the marble counter to pump the poor man's hand, G-Man boomed:

"Oh, really? You got kinfolks in Shaw, Mis'sippi?"

Thanksgiving Dinner - The Easy Way

"Five years ago I felt guilty 'just adding water.'
Now I want to bang the tube against the countertop
and have a five course meal pop out." — Erma Bombeck

Long about holiday time I begin to feel guilty about my aversion to cooking.

I think about my many friends who waltz into the kitchen with smiles on their faces and I marvel. Some people really enjoy the art and pleasure of food preparation, but I look at it as pure drudgery.

Is it fair that Poor Mom must be the one to spend hours and hours and hours concocting delicious dishes for a hungry horde that sweeps in, devours the grub (soup to nuts), and then disappears to sprawl in front of endless TV football games?

Decidedly not.

But the other day my conscience prodded my culinary pitiful self.

Girl, I said to me, you need to hitch your britches and come up with a Thanksgiving meal for all the family. After all, this is what makes memories, right? The family around the table—grandparents, parents, children—all are delighted to be there with the bounty Poor Mom has slaved to prepare in order to nourish her loved ones.

Picture the scene: beaming faces, Dad carving the turkey, Poor Mom in her apron.

(Apron? Yeah, I have one somewhere.)

First of all, I figured I'd better begin with planning the ambiance of the affair.

I'll gather a sack of red and gold autumn leaves out on the driveway, scatter them down the middle of the dining table, then pitch a few ears of Indian corn on the leaves.

I have a little Hallmark Pilgrim woman in a drawer in the kitchen (her little Pilgrim man is long gone. Who knows?), so I'll place her by a cute little pumpkin candle.

Then I'll check for ants . . . and there's my centerpiece, looking good.

Next, linen napkins and placemats will have to be ironed. Silver polished. China and crystal carefully washed.

Or better yet, I'll pull it all out of the cabinet and use as is. Who's going to know?

And then? Oh, yeah. Food. Got to have it.

Well, I'll get Big Star to cook the turkey. Then I'll call the daughters and daughters-in-law.

Jamie can do her wonderful shrimp hors d'oeuvre and a sweet potato casserole.

Katie can do her goat cheese salad and marinated green beans.

Emily can make the dressing and bring the cranberry sauce.

I'll get the caramel cake from the Commons downtown.

Bethany can keep the children out of the kitchen while I'm searching for that apron so I'll look good in the pictures.

See? What a breeze. Once I get organized, cooking for the holidays is not such a difficult thing. Actually, planned well, a holiday meal at my house is not such a burden after all.

It's pretty much "all relative."

Thinking Dumb Thoughts

I'm complaining to my friend Louise about finding time to write during the busy holidays, and she says, "Just write down what you're thinking."

I tell her that could be dangerous.

That night I crawl into bed and notice my alarm clock on the bedside table. The clock has needed new batteries for some time.

"Honey," I say to hubby G-Man, "what time is it? My clock is not right."

G-Man sits up and looks, plops his head back down on the pillow, and says, "Yep. It's ten minutes slow."

"No, it's not that far off," I tell him. "Your clocks are always ten minutes fast."

"I never set my clocks ten minutes fast," he says. "I set them five minutes fast."

I say "Oh." Then I lie there thinking—wondering why he wants to delete even five minutes from his life. The old year is vanishing five minutes early for him while I'm hanging on to every minute.

The next morning I head south to Pike County alone to slather hugs on grandchildren because one has to go to the hospital to have tubes put in his tiny ears. Anesthesia and all that.

I have four hours all by myself to keep thinking.

As I drive I contemplate the landscape. I'm intrigued with green bottles on stakes that march confidently along the edge of every single plowed field I pass. I wonder if the bottles are some sort of signal to extraterrestrial beings, but decide maybe they're intended to be poor men's bottle trees.

I switch on the radio and discover Eric Clapton singing "Going down to the crossroads/down to Rosedale." I think that's definitely cool, but the next song sounds like a bunch of pots and pans tumbling from a kitchen cabinet. I decide to listen instead to an audio book tape—Nevada Barr's "Hunting."

I get to the part where the sheriff says something about "ambient knowledge" and find myself disbelieving. Do sheriffs say stuff like that? Nevada's lost me. I turn it off.

I'm thinking that on four hour trips like this, time is as creeping as cream rising on butter. I'm yawning. Maybe I should stop for a cup of coffee.

I pull off at a Texaco "Gas and Goodies" place, go inside and begin searching for treats to take the grandkids. I spend twenty minutes looking at fuzzy monkeys, china dolls in nauseating pastels, and tee shirts that say, "I love Grandma."

I opt for good ol' M&Ms.

I climb back into the car, take off, then get a mile down the road and realize I wasted twenty minutes and forgot the coffee.

I continue my drive and pass a stretch of fencing, probably a quarter mile of it, white and draped with artificial holly and red plastic bows.

The whole length is festooned still, even though Christmas is over.

"Guess the garland's just hanging around to welcome the new year," I quip aloud, amused at my own wit. Hanging around. Get it?

I'm thinking how I also go the artificial greenery route in my own house. Who has leisure to do more when the hubby subtracts five minutes from every single day?

Numbers take over my brain. Deleting five minutes from every day adds up to almost 2000 less minutes a year—around thirty-three hours out of my life annually. That's a lot of time I could be strewing live greenery, hugging grandkids, replacing clock batteries and doing a dozen other things that need doing.

I frown, realizing after all that calculation that G-Man's method just means I should wake up and start my day five minutes early. I won't.

I flip the radio back on to catch "All Things Considered" on PRM. They're talking about some foot-in-mouth politician. I start looking for another station, deciding I've had enough dumb thoughts on this drive.

I'm thinking it's not always wise to expose what you're thinking, especially when your thinking is stupid—no matter what my friend Louise thinks.

This Name's For You

Here in the south of these United States, naming new babies often involves lots of climbing around in family trees.

Take, for example, the progeny of Gerald, that's G-Man, my husband, and Beth (me), also known as Bebe, both as southern as cornbread and turnip greens. Our eldest is named for her paternal grandfather and both grandmothers; number two daughter is named for me and my sister; number one son is named for his maternal grandfather, his uncle and his father; the lap baby—our end of the line son—is named for his two uncles and his father.

Did I leave anybody out?

We are also able to cover a lot of familial territory with our affinity for double names here in Mississippi and parts close by. Names like Will Tom and James Edward and Mary Edith and Lucy Ann are commonly shortened to nicknames like "Rabbit" and "Cracker" and "Pumpkin" and "Pookie," but everybody knows Lucy Ann, for example, was named for her venerable great-aunts—"Pookie" or no "Pookie."

And in true southern fashion, if the need arises, we aren't averse to stacking names even higher—Jefferson Davis Poindexter Bumpus III is a fictional example (I hope) of a good ole Dixieland moniker that comes ponderously to mind. String 'em out and cover three or four family members, don't you know.

My personal call of bestowal came a couple of years ago.

"Bebe, Bethany went to the doctor this morning and had a sonogram." (This was my wonderful son-in-law Charles calling.)

"Allll right!" I said. "Girl or boy?"

"Another boy."

"Oh, that's great. Wayne needs a brother. They'll have so much fun together."

"We're naming her for you."

"And you've got plenty of hand-me-down clothes, and . . ."

"Bebe, did you hear me? We're naming her for you. I was just kidding—the baby's a girl. We've discussed her name already. She'll have your full name. Given name. Maiden name. The whole works."

Can a heart burst with happiness? Does pride know boundaries? My devoted children were giving me a wonderful gift, and the honor was staggering.

When I placed the phone back in its base, I flopped to the floor. Leaning against the bed, I sat with my eyes closed, trying to imagine what the years would bring for this little Beth. Would she play the piano like her Bebe? Would she string words together like trinkets, as I so love to do? More than likely not. She'll probably be the athlete I always wished I could be, or the cook I'm not, or the president of the United States . . . or any and all of the above.

One thing for certain, she'd have my name, but she'd build her own list of achievements and interests, which is exactly as it should be.

Isn't it confusing having people in the family with the same names?

Not at all. Once you're a grandfather or grandmother you acquire a new name—Granddaddy or Pop or Gran or Nana or something else equally charming. For family purposes and affectionate conversation, I'm just Bebe now.

The only problem this nom d'honeur has caused in my life is the elevation of my meddling inclinations. When I see a young couple about to be parents, I want badly to pull them aside and whisper, "Y'all listen to me. Name that baby for your mamas!"

I wish I could tell these young folks that all the popular fad names in the book could never give their child the sense of precious heritage that only a beloved family name can. And I'd tell them that for a grandparent, an aunt, an uncle, a special friend, there's no more splendid laurel than to have a namesake.

Beth Boswell Dowdy is a precious four-year-old now. She crawls in my lap, gives me a kiss, and says, "Bebe . . . two Beths. You and me." And I melt.

All of Beth's life, you see, when I'm long gone and forgotten by almost everybody else, she'll tell folks, "I was named for my maternal grandmother." And there will probably be many more Beths in our family in the generations to come.

There's something awfully comforting about that.

To Ski Or Not To Ski

Brave, charge ahead folks don't understand people like me. Where they are "no guts, no glory" daredevils, I am prudent, cautious, and just pretty generally chicken-livered.

Hooked on snow skiing over twenty years ago, hubby G-Man still insists we make a Colorado pilgrimage every year, and every year I question his sanity. Am I the only one around those mountains with good sense?

Quite often I see men and women tentatively snow plowing down the slippery slopes. Their skis are wedged tightly, almost as tightly as their lips. Their hands grip poles in a "save me!" posture, and in their bulging eyes I see unadulterated terror. I identify and want to yell at them, "Hey, honey! Give it up. It's OK. You'll be no less a person. Trust me – I'm the consummate non-snow bunny."

Think about it. We don't have snow skiing in the Deep South, so that means we have to travel a great distance to put these boards on our feet and slide, willy nilly, through the snow and ice. We're packed in a condo with the kids, not one of whom can find all the paraphernalia required for hours in the cold – gloves, long johns, turtlenecks, sweaters, insulated jackets, waterproof pants, wool socks – which means somebody, usually mama, has to be the official hunter and sorter. The whole ordeal, including chapped lips and sunburned faces, costs too much money, and I haven't even touched on the pain. And this is fun?

I have long admired the chutzpah of my pal Becky who went skiing for the first time and hated it immediately. In spite of her dislike she advanced beyond Fanny Hill and was taken up the mountain on the chair lift by her instructor. She soon found herself staring over what appeared to her to be an elevator shaft-like cliff.

"I'm not going down that," she said. "Put me back on the chair lift."

"You can't go down on the chair lift," the instructor said. "Nobody does that. You've got to ski down."

"Listen, buster," Becky said, "I rented these skis from your company. If you don't put me on that chair lift I'm going to pitch these blankety-blank skis over that cliff and you can go get 'em."

She rode down on the chair lift.

I reached the same decision finally after ten years in the "Never Ever" beginner classes. I'd gathered enough courage to go with the hot shot members of my family to reaches unknown farther up the mountain, and I snow plowed down the Big Burn with my heart racing ten times faster than my skis.

Wouldn't you know? The others had a ball. "Let's go up and do it again!" they cheered.

Ha! No way was I going to risk life and limb again on the Big Burn.

"No thanks," I said. "I'll make it down to the condo by myself. Y'all go ahead."

I got half-way down and realized I didn't know where in the world I was. Perched on a steep overhang, up to my knees in snow, freezing, I made a vow.

"Lord, if you'll get me down from here I'll never put a pair of skis on my feet ever again."

With tears frozen on my chapped cheeks, nose running, body aching, I finally inched down the mountain, partially on skis but mostly on my derriere. And my little 160 skis have been in the closet ever since.

In my opinion, southern families could save money and spare themselves a lot of hassle by doing this:

*Stay put in the peace and quiet of your own home.

*Turn your air conditioner down to zero.

*Slap yourself upside the head a few times.

*Next, take a big, heavy hammer and whack the living daylights out of your legs. Beat em up good. Get a friend to do the same to your back.

There. You've got the full snow skiing effect at no cost.

If only I could holler at those pitiful folks snow plowing their way down Fanny Hill: "Hey, y'all! Much better is a good slide on a sizable piece of cardboard over on the levee. That's skiing Southern style . . . a mighty fine way to get your thrills. Trust me."

Uniforms – The Answer For Cluttered Closets

Twice a year I do it, and twice a year I vow I will never do it again.

I am sick and tired of changing the clothes hanging in my closet from fall/winter attire to spring/summer attire, back to fall/winter attire, ad infinitum. This is a terrible job and I hate it.

I've been saying for years I'm going to simplify my wardrobe (if what I've got can be classified as wardrobe). As I told some pals the other day, I wear the same three or four things all the time anyway, so what am I doing with all this stuff . . . except transferring it from hall closet to bedroom closet twice a year?

Most of the clothing is two sizes too small and ugly. I have, therefore, reached decision time.

My two oldest grandchildren are in elementary school. While babysitting with them, I've grown to appreciate the ease and comfort of uniforms. Meredith slips into her little white shirt, her plaid jumper with red shorts underneath, her socks and saddle oxfords and she's set to go. Wayne jumps into his khaki pants and green or white shirt, his socks and sneakers, and he's ready.

Meredith's and Wayne's closets are simply arranged and orderly. There are no early morning arguments on school days about what to wear, and there's no keeping up with the Jones kids.

If it works for them, why can't it work for me?

As I cleaned out my jumble of a closet this morning, I was thinking about what kind of uniform an (ahem!) older woman should have. I've got it figured out.

I need:

* 2 pair jeans
* 2 pair black slacks
* 2 pair khaki slacks
* 2 white T-shirts (not Fruit of the Loom)
* 2 black T-shirts (ditto)
* 2 dress shirts/blouses (not fancy)

* 2 neutral colored shift dresses
* 4 dress jackets (for Sundays)
* 2 sweaters (generic)
* 1 sweater (Christmas)
* 1 wedding suit
* 1 funeral suit
* 1 basic party dress (OK, maybe 2)
* 1 working-in-the-yard ensemble
* 1 working-out ensemble (for when and if)
* 1 warm jacket
* 1 long wool coat

To change things up every now and then, I could wear the funeral suit to church or the working-in-the-yard ensemble around the house. That would be nice.

I'll also have a couple of rules. Everything will be mix and match—black, white, khaki, and a red something. No patterns. No flowers. In addition, if I bring in, say, a new Christmas sweater or party dress, I pitch the old one. I'll have only those items on my uniform list and only the allowed number.

And that's the beauty of it all. I'll have only twenty-eight pieces of clothing, more than enough. Imagine the room in my closet. I'll have little to transfer every season and will encounter much less grief. I stress big time now when I extricate something from the tangle of hangers and find it's too wrinkled, little, out-of-date, or uncomfortable.

So the decision has been made. I want a simple, unassuming uniform.

Now, if hubby G-Man would build a closet for me like Bill Gates built his wife with one of those dry-cleaning racks that goes round and round when you punch a button, then I might double up and have more of some things in case of stains. I read that Melinda Gates has forty-two linear feet of rack. That would certainly hold a lot of T-shirts.

Well, I hope my good clothing store friends don't think I'm encouraging people NOT to buy new clothes. Lest they do, let me add this bit of consolation. Nobody's going to follow my lead. This plan is about as obsessive-compulsive as a soul can get, and I don't expect lots of company.

And also, because this uniform wardrobe of mine is a tad bland (akin to plum dowdy), let me assure shopkeepers that I will have to purchase new slacks, T-shirts, and jackets (at least those) every season or, at minimum, twice a year. I'll have to have lots of scarves, funky pins, earrings and bracelets, good-looking shoes and purses, nice belts.

Hoooo-boy! Now I'm excited. I think I'll tackle that closet again, throwing out just about everything in it.

And then I'll go shopping.

Whatcha Lookin' At?

Several of my girlfriends and I were sitting around the other day talking about the way outsiders view Southern women. We're a special breed, there's no question about it.

"A friend in New York told me Southern women are different," I said. "Are we really different?"

"Yep," said my friend Diane. "We're more self conscious."

"Naaa, not me," I said, posturing as a laid-back, do-what-I-want-to kind of gal.

"Well, think about it," Diane said. And we all began to think about it. And discuss it.

"Even if I don't have on any other makeup, I have to wear a bit of lipstick to the grocery store."

"After I take the kids swimming, then leave the pool in my cover-up and want to run in somewhere just for a second, well, I think I've got to go home and get properly dressed."

"And earrings. Got to have my earrings."

On it went—and this is not a pretentious group of ladies, honest.

I sat and listened. The longer I listened, the more I had to face the truth. I'm a self conscious Southern woman.

I can remember when I was a kid I loved the humor of comedian George Gobel. Remember him? Round faced. Innocent. Blessed with hilarious dry wit. I'll never forget Gobel's saying that sometimes he feels like he's "a pair of brown shoes and all the world's a tuxedo." Funny, but true.

Self-conscious. I've never thought of those feelings in that way, but I think Diane was right. She certainly pegged the way I felt a couple of weeks ago at a beautiful wedding here in my town.

While dressing for the wedding I decided on a certain pair of earrings. The earrings hadn't been worn in a while and were missing those little back thingys (hereafter referred to as b.t.'s) into which one pushes the post to secure the earring on the pierced ear. I fished around in my jewelry box and found two loose b.t.'s. They didn't match. One was silver and one was gold.

No problem. Who was going to notice?

Hubby G-Man and I took off for the wedding. Entering the church, we found seats on a row near the back and settled in to gaze at the magnificent sanctuary and the heads in front of us.

Oh, my. The backs of the earlobes of the short haired ladies were lined up like little bitty Thumbelinas decorated with wires and clamps and matching studs. The lobes began to taunt me: "Yoooou don't maa-atch! Yooooou don't maa-atch!"

I was mortified.

Very, very slowly I turned my short haired head to see who was sitting behind me. Brad and Marcie Horton. Well, they were down on the end of their pew; they probably couldn't see the backs of my ears. I twisted a little more to see . . . James Albert Wiggins. Oh, no.

James Albert was sitting right behind me. Because of my short cropped hair there was no way he could miss my silver stud b.t. and my gold stud b.t.

What to do?

The solution was to position my head so the backs of my earlobes weren't showing at the same time. I couldn't turn my head to the left because I'd be facing the wall and wouldn't be able to see the wedding ceremony. So, ever so inconspicuously, I turned my head to the right. Now James Albert could see only the back of the right ear, right?

Bzzzzzzt! Wrong answer.

Well, partially correct. See, it was only a matter of seconds before I got tired of staring at G-Man's left jaw and had to face front again. Thank goodness the wedding started soon after this contortive exercise, and the service was so lovely I totally forgot about my earlobes.

But I can't bear the thought that my tacky b.t.'s might have distracted dear James Albert.

From this moment on I vow I shall always, always make sure my b.t.'s match . . . or maybe I'll just let my hair grow out.

World Peace – One Pair Of Bloomers At A Time

Since most of my newspapers run this column on the Opinion page, I figure every now and then I should express an opinion. Hubby G-Man says no. He says my job is to entertain, not persuade, assure, convince, convert, or opine. But I am the stubborn sort who wants to keep this job, so today I'm going to jump all over this opinion business.

My opinion is that folks would get along a whole heckuva lot better if we still had clotheslines.

Blows my mind to think that the younger generation hardly even knows what a clothesline is. Can't you hear the archeologists generations from now:

"Hey, Mack. Look here. What's this?"

"Oh, you know what that is. That's one of those things people ages ago hung their laundry on to dry. Hard to imagine, huh?"

Well, I think it's a shame our kids will never know the pleasure of securing sweet smelling towels and cloth diapers in neat little rows on the clothesline as the warm sun blesses their whole being. They'll never know the pleasant banter, neighbor to neighbor, across the fence as the laundry hanging proceeds— followed most certainly by a leisurely cup of coffee.

You see, clotheslines helped make good neighbors.

As I reflect on the demise of clotheslines and their value to peaceful relations, I am reminded of the time G-Man and I strung our clothes out a hotel window, mainly to dry them, but, as it turned out, also in a grand gesture of good will.

We had embarked on a vagabond trip to Europe—backpacks and Eurail passes—to see our daughter Bethany who was teaching English in Nagykoros, Hungary. Since we were traveling with backpacks we had only a few changes of clothing, so by the time we reached Vienna we were down to nothing but a bunch of dirties.

"I'm not paying five bucks for the hotel laundry to wash a t-shirt," G-Man fussed. "I can wash everything we got in the bathtub."

I didn't argue. Who cares? So he started scrubbing while my attention went to the gathering crowds outside our fourth floor room's big double window. Strange things were happening on the Blue Danube.

As I helped G-Man string the t-shirts and underwear on a makeshift clothes-line fashioned from the twine of the window blind's pulls, I noticed the crowds were getting thicker. Big ol' stretch limousines were pulling up across the street. On the sidewalk below were guards with guns and all kinds of fawning folks and newspeople with cameras, and many of them were looking our way.

Was our little clothesline attracting the attention of the good citizens of Vienna, Austria? Were we to be the big story for the 6 o'clock TV news-sprecher? Were Viennians sorely missing their clotheslines too?

Well, nein. As the semi-clean laundry frisked at our heads in the balmy Austrian breezes, we perched in the window, exchanging neighborly waves as Jimmy Carter, Warren Christopher, the Dalai Lama, and many more way-up-there honchos exited their limos.

These folks were attending the United Nations' World Conference on Human Rights, see? That's what we found out later.

What you bet after glancing our way they entered that high-falutin' United Nations conference hall with grins on their faces, totally prepared to discuss weighty issues of the world in a calm, harmonious fashion?

Yessir, I'm convinced they did—all because of our neighborly greetings and flip-flapping, sun-soaking, water-dripping, conflict-ripping clothesline.

That's my opinion.

XYZ's of Speaking Southern

"South Mouth . . . is the most charming of American dialects . . . an attempt to 'find and keep the music in American language'. . . melodious . . . [with] relaxed rhythms."
- Robert Hendrickson, *WHISTLIN' DIXIE*

This is an addendum of sorts. The publishers insisted.

"Southerners will understand your expressions," they wrote, "but if this book falls into the hands of one not so geographically blessed, there could be confusion in translation."

Actually that's not really an exact quotation, but it's pretty close to what the publishers said. A glossary was requested, so obviously these kind folks didn't comprehend such Southern Speak as "pizzlesprung," "bootay," and maybe "fallen sisterhood."

Darn. More work for me.

But, ever Miss Agreeable, I scanned the pages of the proofs, searching for obscure phrases and words, a la Dixie, to create a glossary. I couldn't find any obscure phrases and words. Every syllable made sense to me. Wasn't a puzzler in the whole stack of stories.

Here then, dear reader, is my offer: If you find an expression or word that confuses you, write me at bethjacks@hotmail.com. I'll answer and set you straight. I might consider you culturally deprived, but I'll be nice.

The problem is that Southern expressions are as natural to me as breathing. There's nothing foreign about them, so I expect everybody to know them also. You see, I grew up hearing daily the funny phrases of my mother, a whiz with Dixie-isms.

In her late 80s, Mama still spouts expressions that are almost raggedy with frequent use. When we took a trip together recently to a family wedding, I recorded some of her gems. Perhaps several of her quips will help confused readers decipher South Mouth.

* "Honey," Mama said one day, "I don't know most of the folks at this wedding from Adam's housecat."

We Southerners all know what she meant, but for the Yankees who might be listening, Mama was giving her version of "I wouldn't know 'em from Adam's off ox," referring, linguist Robert Hendrickson says, to the "off" ox in the yoke farthest away from the driver. This is a variation of "I wouldn't know him from Adam," which isn't much good, Hendrickson points out, since most of us wouldn't have a bit of trouble recognizing a fellow playing peekaboo in naught but a fig leaf.

* "I realize my hair looks terrible," Mama told us before the bridesmaids luncheon, "but all I could do was give it a lick and a promise."

She brushed her hair quickly, according to Hendrickson's definitions, and vowed to spend more time in curlers later. An entertaining book called WHY DO WE SAY IT? (Castle Books) contends the "lick" probably comes from the "licking into shape" a mama bear gives her newborn cubs. That's probably not right, but it's real sweet.

* Answering the question, "How you feeling this morning, Mama?", she answered, "Fair to middling, and how's your corporosity?"

Corporosity is an old-fashioned term, Hendrickson writes, for one's body or state of health, probably deriving from corpulence, of which our husky family has plenty. (I can hear my sisters protest—with good humor, of course—"Speak for your cotton-pickin' self, blabber mouth.")

* "My goodness," said Mama, observing the passel of great-grandchildren, "they're darlin', but they sure are full of beans."

No, she wasn't referring to gaseous, although that wouldn't have been far off the mark. Beans have long been considered energy producers, and believe me, those kids were definitely about as "full of beans" as any chilluns cooped up in a hotel could be. Let's just say they were extraordinarily energized.

* "I'll swanee, Little Jack is the spittin' image of his Uncle Jack," Mama said about her great-grandson, curly-haired Jack Beckham.

"Spittin' image?" WHY DO WE SAY IT? explains this expression is a corruption of an earlier phrase, "the very spit and image," referring to two people so similar one could have been spit from the other's mouth. Ptooey!

* "Did you see the tall gal down in the lobby?" Mama asked. "She was naked as a boiled chicken."

Self-explanatory, this one. And the gal was.

* Saving the best for last, Mama declared at the wedding reception that "she hadn't had such fun since the hogs ate grandma."

I'm not touching that. Mama's the only one with enough snap in her garters to talk about porkies gobbling granny-women—and she did have one rip roodle of a time.

So I ask you, how could I be exposed to language like that and not absorb it like cornbread in pot liquor?

Oh yeah, "pizzlesprung," "bootay," and "fallen sisterhood"? Well, "pizzlesprung" means absolutely, positively worn to a frazzle. "Bootay" is Southern semi-French for rump. "Fallen sisterhood" refers to those girls your mama didn't want your big brother bringing around the house.

Are there more? Write me.

The time has come to quit piddling around and send this book to press, but I challenge readers to keep the music of Southern Speak flowing. It's a heritage thing—a Dixie duty, as one sorry poet put it, "to our latitudes of lovely languor."

Thanks for reading my stories. Mama would be pleased as a possum that you spent time with my foolishment.

Pax.

About the Author

Author of *Grit, Guts, and Baseball,* Beth Boswell Jacks is a weekly personal essay/humor columnist for a number of Southern newspapers. Her verse is published frequently in children's magazines, and she is also the editor of USADEEPSOUTH.COM. Jacks lives in the Mississippi Delta with G-Man and Pharaoh.

Printed in the United States
17318LVS00004B/106-2010